I0578559

Published by: Cinnabar Moth Publishing LLC
Santa Fe, New Mexico

Cover Design by: MiblArt

ISBN-13: 978-1-953971-12-8
Library of Congress Control Number: 2021941959

Relatively Normal Secrets

C.W. ALLEN

Chapter 1

ADULTS, AND THEIR PECULIARITIES

This had better be important. Zed knew it wouldn't be, though. It never was.

He plucked his way dutifully up the rungs of the swaying rope ladder. After all, he had agreed to the pact, and that was that. If either of them called a meeting, for any reason, the other was honor-bound to attend. Even if it meant putting down your book right when you were getting to the good part. Sometimes it hurt to have principles.

"All right, I'm here," he grumbled, hoisting himself onto the weathered slats of the treehouse floor and extracting his official meeting notebook from his pocket. "What's so urgent it couldn't wait until I hit a chapter break? I think I've figured out who the Sunset Towers bomber is, but now I'm going to have to re-read that last—"

"This is much more important than your silly book!" his sister scoffed. "We have a real mystery on our hands! Prepare to take some serious notes—you are not going to want to miss the Grade A Prime evidence I've got lined up."

"Not again," he groaned. "For the last time, Tuesday, we were not adopted! And even if we were—which obviously, we weren't—that's not a problem, and Mom and Dad wouldn't hide it from us!" Zed slumped back against the guardrail and settled in. Might as well get comfortable; this was going to take a while. It always did when she got on a roll.

Tuesday flung a Pop Tart at him like a Frisbee and smirked as he caught it (mostly to prevent it from colliding with his face). "Can't argue when you're chewing!" she said. "I've got it all figured out this time, really, just listen."

Zed nibbled off the corners in sullen silence while his sister launched into her prepared speech. He allowed the words to wash over his ears without fully making contact with his brain, like a stream slipping around a submerged stone. It wasn't really her fault, he thought, nodding along to Tuesday's feverish explanations. Maybe she could have made peace with their parents' eccentricities, if it hadn't been for her name.

He suspected Tuesday was secretly rather fond of her first name; unusual, to be sure, but it had a certain quirky appeal. "June" was a solid, traditional choice for a middle name; "Tuesday June" rolled off the tongue rather nicely. But making her way through life with a name like

"Tuesday June Furst" (especially when she had been born on Saturday March Eleventh) was apparently more than his sister could bear. Zed was, naturally, sworn to silence on this point. Tuesday claimed she was only two years old when she first realized there was anything humorous about her particular assortment of names and had devoted the entire decade that followed to keeping the middle one a secret.

Zed had fared only slightly better in that department. Mostly, people assumed he had been given an old family name—short for Zedekiah, perhaps. But no, it was just Zed. In fact, people asked so often whether it was a nickname that he'd developed the habit of introducing himself as "just Zed." That usually fended off the more personal follow-up questions, but not the well-meaning adults gleefully informing him, for the four thousandth time, that his name was the letter Z in some parts of the world. People always brought it up whenever he introduced himself, as though a ten-year-old boy couldn't possibly have heard about it before, and they were treating him to a delicious new morsel of trivia he would treasure forever. Why were adults so obsessed with dissecting and analyzing names? As far as Zed was concerned, a name is just a collection of sounds you yell at someone when you want their attention. At least his parents had not given him any middle name at all, so he didn't have to explain even more sounds to adults he met for the first time.

Having eaten several revolutions around the edges of the pastry, Zed found himself left with the final jammy bite in the center. He popped it into his mouth and licked his fingers clean while his mind shifted off auto pilot and tuned back into his sister's ranting.

The topic of today's Paranoia Lecture turned out to be their dog. Or, more accurately, their mother's dog. Whether Tuesday was more concerned with the dog itself, or their mother's obsession with it, was up for debate. But Zed had to admit that, for once, his sister had identified a shred of evidence worth considering: the dog was definitely a problem. On that point, everyone agreed. Everyone, that is, except Zora Furst.

Their mother had acquired Nyx before Tuesday and Zed were born. Their father was fond of saying the dog had not managed to learn anything in the years that followed, but that was not strictly true. While it was true that she did not come when called or sit on command, the dog had in fact learned many tricks. Nyx had learned quite early on, for example, how to help herself to the contents of the refrigerator. No one was quite sure how an animal without thumbs was capable of opening a refrigerator door, since she had never been caught in the act, but an entire ham doesn't simply get up and go for a stroll during the night, now does it?

Zed imagined some people would consider it normal to take a dog along to run errands—as long as the dog could fit comfortably inside a purse, that is, or at the very least wait patiently in the car. But Nyx was neither tiny, nor well-behaved and patient. She was, in fact, huge. Her bristly black fur and legs that seemed much too long for the rest of her frame made her look like a gigantic hairy spider. His mother spent nearly every moment in the dog's company, and whenever she needed to go inside the grocery store, or post office, or other location where dogs are generally unwelcome, she brought Nyx along to wait in the car for her return. Nyx made use of this time by bouncing anxiously from seat to seat, smearing her nose on the windows.

It must be noted that while animal rights activists would strongly advise against leaving a dog locked in a car for any length of time, Nyx was never in any danger. In the first place, the car was never locked; while Zed felt that the most dangerous thing about the dog was her habit of claiming unattended sandwiches, her appearance was intimidating enough to make even the most determined burglar suddenly remember an urgent appointment anywhere but there. Secondly, and perhaps more to the point, Nyx had also taught herself how to operate all the car's buttons and knobs. Whenever he and Tuesday finished errands with their mother and returned to the car, they invariably found Nyx with her nose inches from a blasting air conditioner, the radio station blaring opera, or polka—pretty much any musical style other than the sort they had chosen on the ride there. Zed was fairly certain most vehicles required the engine to be turned on to run the air conditioner, but his mother dismissed this as a safety feature.

Mrs. Furst simply refused to entertain the idea that Nyx was anything other than the finest specimen ever produced by caninekind. This was a surprisingly easy opinion for her to maintain, because Nyx was always on her best behavior whenever Mrs. Furst was around. When greeting Mrs. Furst, Nyx sat obediently, raising her chin to the perfect angle to produce a dignified profile while waiting for a pat on the head. She always seemed to have her back turned when Nyx greeted Mr. Furst by draping her paws over his shoulders and restyling the left side of his hair with her tongue. Since Zed and Tuesday were nowhere near as tall as their father, the dog's customary greeting usually left them flat on their backs while Nyx licked their faces.

Despite the fact that Nyx didn't know her own strength and never followed commands of any kind, Zed and Tuesday were actually quite attached to their dog. Not nearly as attached as Mrs. Furst was, of course, but the children already knew their parents' behavior was even less rational than that of most adults. What all this proved to Tuesday was not really clear, from her argument. Most of her arguments seemed to boil down to "our parents are weird and must therefore be up to something."

"All adults are weird!" Zed protested. "They're always losing their car keys, and wake up every morning looking like zombies, and can't ever call you the right name on the first try. That doesn't mean they're hiding some vast conspiracy!"

"All right then," Tuesday snapped, "let's go ask all our relatives if Mom and Dad have always acted this sketchy. Oh wait—we don't have any."

Zed had to admit this was unusual. None of his friends' parents had balked at the My Family Tree homework sheet he'd brought home from school last year. Mr. and Mrs. Furst had flatly refused to help Zed fill his out, claiming they had no extended family. Zed had tried to point out that this was impossible—everyone must have had some family, once—but when he insisted there must be some grandparents or aunts or third cousins twice removed, his parents abruptly shut the conversation down, and he was left to bluff his way through the assignment. He already knew there were no photographs to cut up and paste to it—none that he'd ever seen anyway—but he had at least hoped for some names to put to the faces he could only imagine.

Still, having been adopted was out of the question, as was having been kidnapped from a grocery store or playground as infants (this was Tuesday's next idea).

Tuesday wore the dark sheen of her father's hair and the determined set of his jaw as plainly as if she'd taken them out of his closet one day and tried them on for size. Zed shared his mother's love of mystery novels and jigsaw puzzles, her long straight nose, and the loose waves of her hair, exactly the color of maple syrup. No, Zed insisted, backing down the rope ladder of the Meeting Tree to return to his book, they could not possibly have been adopted (or stolen). Nor could their parents be secret agents, or in a witness protection program, or any other of Tuesday's outrageous theories.

If only Tuesday's theories had been just a bit more outrageous, they might have come closer to the truth.

EXCERPT FROM ZED'S NOTEBOOK
Hypothesis:
Mom and Dad are hiding something

Tuesday's "Clues"
- ~~Gave us weird names~~ (get over it!)
- ~~Obsessed with Nyx~~ (everyone needs a hobby)
- ~~Nyx is weird too~~ (what's that got to do with Mom and Dad?)
- No old photos (maybe, see explanations below)
- No relatives (impossible, but see below)
Tuesday's "Possible" "Explanations"
- They're really:

o ~~Aliens~~ (someone's been watching too much late-night TV)

o ~~Secret agents~~ (see above)

o ~~In Witness Protection~~ (see both of above)

o ~~Kidnappers on the run~~ (someone's been watching too much cable news)

More Likely Explanations
- Prefer minimalist decoration
- Family photos destroyed by:
o Fire
o Flood
o Tornado
o Improper archival storage
o Lost during a move
- Family feud, don't speak to relatives
- Neither had siblings
- Parents died of totally normal causes, like old age or lumbago

Zed's Official Conclusion:
Tuesday is a drama queen, who should really:
- Read more
- Or get a hobby (other than "being suspicious")
- Or play outside
- Or make some friends

Chapter 2

ARDEN FURST, WORKER

Despite her attention to every odd thing they did in her presence, Tuesday had never wondered much about what her parents were up to when she wasn't around to supervise. Mrs. Furst was a homemaker, so Tuesday assumed that while she and Zed were at school, their mother was busy with tasks like folding socks, or preparing dinner, or scrubbing dog drool off of Nyx's favorite sofa cushion. Mr. Furst went to Work. He left for Work immediately after breakfast in the morning, and just before dinner he arrived Home From Work. In between those two events, clearly he was At Work. But Tuesday had never given any thought to what he actually did there. Never, that is, until her teacher, Ms. Plimstock, assigned the class to write a report on their parents' professions.

To introduce the assignment, Ms. Plimstock called on a few students and asked them about their parents' job titles. Joey Blumfield's mother was a lawyer. Alice Chen's father was an advertising executive. Evan Murphy's parents ran their own bakery. But then Ms. Plimstock had squinted out over the class, her spectacles slipping down her long beaky nose, to select one more student.

"Tuesday," Ms. Plimstock clucked, "what about your parents?"

Tuesday felt a fleeting zap in her chest, which buzzed along her arms and out through her fingertips. She hated being called on in class. It was fine when she raised her hand, when she already had a comment prepared—but being interrogated out of the blue felt a lot like being shot in the back by a sniper. Not that this had ever happened to Tuesday, of course, but she was certain the sensation must be similar.

"Ummm…well…my Mom takes care of the house, and my Dad goes to Work." This elicited a few unsympathetic giggles from her classmates.

"Yes dear, but what does your father do?" Ms. Plimstock prodded impatiently.

Tuesday wasn't able to give any satisfactory answer. Ms. Plimstock moved on, but Tuesday's classmates grinned and stowed that tidbit away to revisit later.

At lunch, her father was the headlining topic of conversation. Perhaps, everyone joked, he was some kind of secret agent—if anyone found out what he really did all day, he'd have to erase their memories or have them deported to Jupiter. Tuesday made a hasty decision: better to ride the wave of laughter, than drown in it. This was ridiculous, of course!

Of course it was.

Tuesday heaved her backpack onto the lunch table and made a production of searching for a missing paper until the cafeteria's collective attention bounded on to a new distraction. She retrieved last week's History assignment and tried to look intensely interested in reviewing it, staring through the page with unfocused eyes while zoning out to the satisfying snapping sound her carrot sticks made, the pitch falling rhythmically as her teeth chopped each one shorter and shorter.

The newly-hatched suspicions about her parents' routines burrowed in with the rest of the doubts nesting in her brain. It wasn't just the way they sidestepped any mention of their lives before they had children. It wasn't just their odd taste in names. It was just—oh, everything.

Her last name should have been different, for one thing; Tuesday was sure of it. Her father wouldn't say what it might have been, but anything else would have been fine with her, really. Anything that wouldn't make her a walking punchline. If her parents hadn't been so weird, her mother would have taken her father's last name when they got married, like normal people. Then Tuesday could have inherited his name, instead of just his face. But no, they had decided to buck tradition and do the operation the other way around. Tuesday had tried, time and again, to explain to her mother how strange this was—none of her friends' fathers had changed their names, that was just absurd! Her mother's response was always the same: "Is it?"

Tuesday wasn't sure whether her mother was trying to make some kind of point, or was just hopelessly clueless, but she was sure of one thing—the conversation always ended there. Perhaps, Tuesday imagined, if her family lived in one of the carefully curated subdivisions her friends came home to every day, all sculpted and polished and pruned into shape, the other things wouldn't stick out so much. Instead, the school bus rumbled right past these fortresses of normality, way out to the edge of town, and deposited her at the end of a long, twisty gravel drive emerging from the woods.

"Your friends don't get to listen to owls at night," her father often argued, "and it must be awfully hard to see the stars behind all those streetlights." Tuesday knew, though—in middle school, you only get one pass for being different, maybe two if you're lucky, and hers was already used up on a calendar pun.

"Being different is a gift," her mother always said.

Tuesday wished this one had come with a receipt.

At precisely 6:02 that evening, Mr. Furst arrived Home From Work. He strolled in the back door, an umbrella hooked over one arm.

"So Dad, how was work?" Tuesday called from the sofa.

"Fine," her father replied.

"You know Dad, every time you ask me how school was, and I answer 'fine,' you roll your eyes and demand more details," Tuesday pointed out.

Mr. Furst hung his jacket in the hall closet and returned his umbrella to its stand by the front door. He stared at it for a moment, lost in thought, before tearing his eyes away to return Tuesday's comically accusatory stare. "Fair enough," he agreed. "What do you want to know?"

At that moment Nyx bounded into the room and leaped up to greet Mr. Furst. When standing on her back legs, Nyx was just as tall as Mr. Furst—slightly taller, in fact. They looked just like a couple dancing, except most women don't attempt to lick the ears off of their dance partners. It took several moments to fend off Nyx's enthusiasm, and then Mr. Furst immediately excused himself to wash off the dog slobber that was now trickling down his neck.

Next Tuesday intercepted him in the bathroom hallway, a damp towel still draped over his shoulders, heading toward his bedroom.

"Dad, I—" was all she had time to get out before her father interrupted.

"Just a minute Tuesday, I need to change into a fresh shirt."

She waited outside the bedroom door, arms crossed, one foot tapping impatiently. When the door opened and Mr. Furst emerged (in a clean shirt, and without the towel) he found himself nose to nose with his daughter. He blinked.

"Tuesday, did you drag a chair all the way from the kitchen just so you could stare me down when I opened the door?"

"I'll ask the questions here!" Tuesday snapped playfully, still perched on the chair she had, indeed, dragged down the hall for that very purpose. "Are you avoiding me? Wait, don't answer that. Back to the point. When you go to work, what do you do?"

"Dinner's ready!" Mrs. Furst called.

Without a word Mr. Furst tucked Tuesday under his arm like a football and headed for the kitchen. The legs of her chair etched parallel tracks into the carpet as Mr. Furst dragged it along with his free hand. Normally Tuesday liked a good roughhousing bout with her father (moms never seem to be up for that sort of thing), but this time she suspected she was being deliberately thwarted. Mr. Furst returned the chair to its place at the table and plunked Tuesday down in it.

Zed was already seated at the table, and Mrs. Furst was busy ladling mashed potatoes onto everyone's plates.

"How was your day, Arden?" she asked as her husband pecked her on the cheek and took his seat.

"Yes, Dad, how was your day?" Tuesday interjected. "What specific tasks occupied your time? In detail."

Zed was certain his parents exchanged the briefest of meaningful glances. But he was even more certain that encouraging his sister when she was already on a roll was both unnecessary and possibly hazardous, so he kept this observation to himself.

"You know, I don't think you've ever discussed your work much with the children," Mrs. Furst commented placidly. "Why don't you tell them more about it?"

Mr. Furst chewed a bite of broccoli, thinking. "I'm a consultant for a security company," he answered at last. "I help keep people safe."

"You mean like a bodyguard?" Zed asked.

"No," Mr. Furst answered (a little too quickly, Zed thought). "No. Of course not. Although I suppose you could call some of the people I work with 'bodyguards.' I help people who feel they need extra security decide on a plan that will keep them safest. I look at their home, workplace, and routine and suggest changes I can help them make. That might mean better locks on their doors, or lights around their office at night, or in some cases, they may want to hire a 'personal security specialist' to accompany them when they go out in public."

"What kind of people?" Tuesday probed. "Like celebrities? Billionaires? Royalty?"

"There's no royalty around here," Zed pointed out. "Unless you count Don the Mattress King from the TV commercials."

Tuesday didn't. She stuck her tongue out at him.

Their father laughed. "Most of my clients are fairly ordinary people. While some may have more reason than others to be concerned about their security, everyone deserves to feel safe, don't you think?"

While Zed pondered that over a forkful of potatoes, Mrs. Furst turned to Tuesday. "A lady uses her tongue to speak wisdom and truth, not taunt those who disagree with her."

"Good thing I'm not one, then," Tuesday mumbled. She crumpled moodily back into her chair, just in time to glimpse Nyx liberating the pork chop from her plate. No one else seemed to have noticed. With a 'glorp', the evidence vanished down the dog's gullet.

"If only my children were as naturally well-mannered as my dog," Mrs. Furst crooned to Nyx, who had sidled up to her chair. Nyx licked her lips noisily.

With the mystery resolved, Tuesday wrote her report, and Ms. Plimstock's seventh grade class remained secure in the knowledge that Tuesday's family was blissfully ordinary. Apparently teachers spend their lunch hour in the breakroom plotting, because two weeks later, Zed was given an identical assignment. He didn't mind, though. Reporting on his father's completely normal job was nothing compared to the effort it had taken to persuade Tuesday that their father had not, in fact, learned his trade through his secret past as a master criminal.

Chapter 3

A FIRST TIME FOR EVERYTHING

Every day after school, Zed came in the front door, slipped off his backpack and shoes, and wandered into the kitchen in search of a snack. Every day, on his way to the kitchen, he passed the living room, where Nyx sprawled over the length of the sofa, sleeping on her back with her spindly legs dangling in the air. Every day, as he passed this sight in the living room, he shook his head and chuckled to himself that the dog's preferred posture resembled an enormous dead cockroach. And every day, Nyx would blink a sleepy eye at Zed, yawn, then scramble off the sofa and follow him to the kitchen just in case his snack might generate any stray crumbs that required her attention. These things happened every school day, which was why Zed felt so uneasy when he arrived home one sun-drenched September afternoon with the sense that something—though he could not quite put his finger on exactly what—was different. The front door had been locked, as usual. Nothing seemed out of order in the front hall. All was quiet. But Nyx was not on the sofa.

"Hello?" he called down the echoing hallway. "Mom? You home? Is everything all right?"

"In here, dear!" His mother's voice rang out from the back of the house.

Zed followed the voice to his parents' bedroom. Mrs. Furst was kneeling over a small satchel, rearranging whatever was inside. Nyx snuffled her snout down into the depths of the bag. "Ah, there you are, Zed!" she said brightly. "Nyx was just helping me pack."

"Pack what?" Zed asked. "Are you going somewhere?"

"Dad has to go on a last-minute business trip, and he asked me to go with him."

"Why?"

"Well why not?" his mother laughed. "I don't exactly need permission to spend time with your father, do I?"

"I didn't mean that," Zed faltered. What did he mean, anyway? "It's just…you've never gone with Dad on business trips before."

"Well, there's a first time for everything. It will only be for a couple of days. You and Tuesday are going to stay next door with Mrs. Alvarez until we get back. You'll be at school most of the time anyway—you'll hardly notice we're gone."

Zed doubted that. For one thing, unless Nyx was also invited along on this trip (unlikely), the dog was bound to spend the next two days pacing and whining incessantly. Nyx was rarely more than a few steps away from his mother, and any time they had to be separated for even a few minutes the dog fretted as if Mrs. Furst had been kidnapped by pirates or something. Two whole days might cause her a complete meltdown, which would be hard to ignore. It wasn't so much that Zed minded his parents leaving—after all, Mrs. Alvarez was a sweet old lady who had been their neighbor his entire life, and had been delighted to watch them for shorter periods of time on many occasions. She'd probably spend the whole time insisting they eat third helpings of empanadas and hot chocolate. And his mother was right, they would be at school most of the time anyway. It was just…something didn't seem right.

If Zed had expected his sister to share his misgivings, he was wrong. When Tuesday stepped off the middle school bus twenty minutes later and Zed informed her they'd be spending the next two days with Mrs. Alvarez, she acted like Christmas had come early. "Yes!" she gushed, punching the air in celebration. "Empanada time!"

"And you're not even the least bit curious where they're going?" Zed asked.

Tuesday waved a hand, swatting Zed's concerns away like irritating insects. "What part of 'business trip' are you unclear on? Dad's probably going to a conference, or interviewing new deadbolt suppliers, or something boring like that. Mom gets to go sightseeing and hang out in the hotel, and when he's done for the day they'll go to a fancy restaurant and eat snails. Boring grownup stuff."

"Mom's not taking the dog." Zed dangled this observation in front of Tuesday like raw meat over a piranha tank. Of all the times Tuesday had raised suspicion over ordinary things, why couldn't she just take the bait when there was actually something to be skeptical about?

"Well of course she can't take Nyx with her," Tuesday agreed, slowly. She sounded less confident now.

"She's never done that before," Zed further observed.

"I suppose it is a tad out of character."

"Mom won't even walk to the end of the driveway to check the mailbox unless Nyx comes with her. Dad had to talk Mom out of trying to smuggle her into a movie theater once! On their anniversary. But now she's going to leave town for days without a care in the world? We're not getting the whole story."

"But what do you expect to do about it?" Tuesday argued, exasperated. "Are you planning to call Mom out on it? Accuse her of lying? Demand she tell you where they're really going, because a 'business trip' is just too far-fetched to be believed? Honestly," she finished with a sly grin, "you're starting to sound like me."

"What do you suggest then?" Zed shot back. He resented the idea that Tuesday, for once, was serving as the voice of reason. But he just couldn't shake the knotted feeling in his stomach. This was like trying to force together two puzzle pieces that almost fit, but not quite. He couldn't explain why, but something was definitely wrong.

"I suppose we could go check the bag she packed," Tuesday conceded. "Maybe she's taking something with her that will give us a clue."

While Tuesday stationed herself at the kitchen table and insisted she needed her mother's help with her homework, Zed stole into his parents' bedroom. After a brief search, he located her bag next to the clothes hamper behind the bedroom door. It was not a typical suitcase, but rather a plain leather satchel. He lifted the flap and rifled through the bag's contents, his eyes searching hungrily for a hotel reservation paper, unusual accessories—anything that might provide a clue about his parents' destination.

Everything inside was disappointingly ordinary. A set of pajamas, a couple of shirts and a pair of jeans, a shiny, pointy pair of high heeled shoes, her favorite green dress—nothing at all that would seem out of place on a business trip. His father was not home yet, but Zed discovered his mother had already packed a similar leather bag for him: two striped button-down shirts, three ties, shaving cream and a razor, socks.

Rats! Maybe he was just imagining things…

Zed placed the bags back behind the door, scanned the room to make sure he had not left anything behind, and crept back out of the room as silently as he had come. He did not feel any less wary than he had an hour ago—in fact, the lack of proof somehow strengthened his suspicions—but he didn't know what else he could do. He resolved to wait things out for the time being and see if any further evidence presented itself.

Hypothesis:
Mom and Dad are hiding something

Zed's Clues
- Dad's never gone on business trips before (why now?)
- Mom's never gone with him (because he never goes anywhere)
- Not taking the dog (Mom ALWAYS takes the dog. EVERYWHERE.)
- Won't say where the trip is to (why not?)
- Won't say what the trip is for ("business" doesn't count)
- Packed totally normal luggage (diversion?)

Tuesday's "Possible" "Explanations"
- They're really:
  - ~~Boring adults~~ (where's the Drama Queen when I need her?)
  - ~~Doing exactly what they claim~~ (see above)
  - ~~Who don't need their children's approval~~ (see both of above)
  - ~~Who cares, empanada party!~~ (focus, Tuesday!)

  More Likely Explanations
- ~~Mafia?~~
- ~~Corporate espionage?~~
- ~~Secret mission of supreme importance?~~
- ~~Romantic getaway?~~

Zed's Official Conclusion:
VERY SUSPICIOUS. NEED MORE DATA.

"The kids suspect something," Mrs. Furst sighed to her husband as she set the bags she had packed that afternoon onto the bed. She removed everything inside and carefully returned each item to its place in the closet. She then lifted three loose floorboards from the closet floor, and from the cavity beneath retrieved a wooden box. Dust coated every inch of its surface as thoroughly as frosting on a cake.

"Well of course they do, they're not stupid," Mr. Furst replied. "I'd be disappointed if they hadn't checked our luggage."

"Don't you feel a bit guilty about deceiving them?"

"Hey, every word we told them was the truth. We have business, and we're going on a trip to take care of it. Beyond that, the less they know, the better."

Mrs. Furst gingerly lifted the lid from the box, sending a plume of dust spiraling through the air. One by one she removed the contents of the box and distributed them between the two bags: two dirty, worn, hooded cloaks; two folded bundles of clothing; a handful of strange copper coins with holes through the middle, strung on a metal loop; a tarnished brass compass; and finally, a gold ring. This last item she inspected thoughtfully, rather than placing it in her bag with the others. It gleamed in stark contrast to the other items that had emerged from the box, as shiny and pristine as the others were battered. Where some rings might have held a gemstone, this had instead a flat surface engraved with an image of two intertwined birds.

She coaxed the wedding ring off her finger, then strung it alongside the engraved ring onto a long necklace. She put the necklace on and tucked it under her shirt.

"Do you really think you're going to need that, Zora?" Mr. Furst asked.

"I hope not," she sighed, "but I suppose we'll know soon enough."

Chapter 4
TRUTH AND CONSEQUENCES

Breakfast in the Furst household was typically a somber affair, with pajama-clad diners munching soggy corn flakes while reading the back of the cereal box, or drowsily buttering toast. This morning was not a typical morning, however. Mr. and Mrs. Furst had risen early and had already dressed and eaten by the time Tuesday trudged into the kitchen to rifle through the pantry in search of the Chocolate Cannonball Crunch her mother kept trying to hide behind the Bran Brix. She was seven spoonfuls in before she remembered Zed had charged her with prying more details out of their parents before they left on their "business trip." Zed, meanwhile, awoke calm but vigilant, determined not to let any potential hint to their plans slip by him. He settled into a strategic position at the table, with a good view of his mother busy in the kitchen and his father reading the newspaper. Zed shook his head. Who reads a newspaper anymore, anyway?

"So…" Tuesday ventured awkwardly. "Big day today, huh Mom?"

"Not really," Mrs. Furst said over her shoulder as she bustled about stuffing sandwiches into their lunch bags. "I took care of all the packing yesterday. We're ready to head out as soon as we see you off to school." She gestured in the direction of the luggage lined up against the wall near the front door.

"I don't think you mentioned what city your trip is to," Tuesday tried.

"No, I probably didn't," her mother replied simply.

Tuesday allowed her unasked question to hang in the air, hoping the stale silence would goad someone into an explanation. Mrs. Furst continued spreading peanut butter without looking up.

"It's a small town," Mr. Furst offered, at last. "I doubt you've heard of it."

Zed and Tuesday exchanged glances. Their parents pretended not to notice. It was like some bizarre card game, with each player silently stewing in the knowledge that the others are concealing something, each waiting to pounce on any potential clue, each painfully aware their every move is being analyzed.

The spell was broken as Nyx bounded into the room with a tennis ball in her mouth. She dropped it unceremoniously in Mr. Furst's lap and waited for him to throw it. He stood to wipe off the wet spot the slobbery toy had created on his trousers; the tennis ball dropped to the floor and rolled away. Determining the trousers a lost cause, he headed for the bedroom to change, muttering under his breath.

Zed motioned to Tuesday, and they set off to their rooms to finish getting ready for school.

"Drat! We didn't learn anything new at all!" Tuesday hissed to Zed when they were alone in the hall.

"Sure we did," he whispered back. "They're definitely dodging our questions, which means they're up to something. And they didn't ask why you were asking so many questions, which means they know we're up to something."

The atmosphere was so strained that in the end, Zed and Tuesday were relieved when their mother declared it was time to leave. She and Mr. Furst collected their bags and ushered everyone to the driveway to wait for the school bus. Mr. Furst started to pull the front door closed behind him, but abruptly returned to retrieve his umbrella. "Can't forget this," he murmured.

"What do you need your umbrella for?" Zed asked as they crunched down the gravel path. "It's not supposed to rain today."

"Oh, just in case," Mr. Furst replied. "You never know when it might come in handy."

FURST FAMILY SAFETY RULES
As related by Dad, recorded by Zed

- Don't talk to strangers (duh)
- Don't give out personal information (see above)
- Consider all available resources (see below)
- Everything can be a tool
- Always know where the exits are (fire safety?)
- Don't open the door unless you already know who's there
- If all else fails, run to the Meeting Tree

The day seemed to Tuesday to last forever. Once, when she glanced at the clock above the chalkboard for the hundredth time, she was convinced the hands had actually crept backward a few minutes. When the bell rang at the end of her final class, she sprinted all the way to the bus, completely forgetting that her own haste could not make the bus arrive at her house any sooner.

Zed was already home when Tuesday arrived, and seemed to have the same plan in mind. With their parents gone, no one would be around to obstruct their "data collection" efforts. That was what Zed called it anyway, but Tuesday preferred not to sugarcoat things; they wanted to snoop.

"What are we even looking for?" Tuesday grumbled, rummaging underneath their parents' bed. "All I'm finding are dust bunnies."

"I'm not sure," Zed replied, "but I'll know it when I see it." He hated to admit it, but their search was turning up nothing. Nyx crouched down beside them and looked under the bed too. Her wagging tail kept thumping Zed in the back.

Zed was about to give up and suggest they head over to Mrs. Alvarez's house when the doorbell rang. Tuesday, startled, smacked her head on the underside of the bed frame. She sat up, massaging her injured skull.

"I'll get it," she told Zed. "You keep looking." She ambled down the hall, Nyx at her heels, still rubbing the sore spot on the back of her head.

Mr. Furst, being a security expert, had impressed many safety rules on his children. One was, "always know your exits." Another was, "consider all your resources." And yet another was, "know who's on the other side of the door before you open it." Usually Tuesday was very conscientious. But today, perhaps because her mind was on the unsuccessful evidence hunt (or perhaps the knot on her head), Tuesday threw the door open without so much as a peep through the window beforehand. And if she had looked first, things might have gone very differently.

Tuesday had expected to find Mrs. Alvarez behind the door, come to fetch them when they had not arrived promptly after school, or perhaps Girl Scouts selling cookies. These were definitely not Girl Scouts. She opened the door and found herself staring up at two very large men standing shoulder to shoulder on the porch. They were dressed in the sort of jumpsuits garbage collectors or cable repairmen wear. The man on the left—tall, heavy, and bearded—clutched a two-way radio in one hand. The man on the right—thinner, with wild eyebrows and lips curled into a sinister sneer—held a metal clipboard.

"Is your father home?" the eyebrow man asked. There was a hint of wicked laughter in his voice, as though he already knew the answer.

Tuesday's heart plummeted into her stomach. She had messed up, and she knew it.

"Sure, I'll go get him," she lied, trying hard to look composed. She attempted to close and bolt the door.

"Nice try, pigeon," the bearded man growled, and he pushed his way through.

Zed came around the corner to see what was going on. He glanced from the men barging through the front door, to Tuesday, backing up slowly with a horrified expression on her face. Without a word he snatched Tuesday's hand and began to tug her toward the back door.

Nyx, who had been behind Tuesday in the hall when the door opened, darted between the men and Tuesday. Her body flattened nearly to the ground, her ears slicked back, the ruff of fur on the back of her neck sprang into a mohawk. A deep, echoing growl rumbled from her throat.

Zed and Tuesday did not notice any kind of transition. All they knew was, one moment the men were holding a radio and a clipboard, and the next, they had turned their attention to Nyx; Eyebrow Man was now gripping a long, curved sword, and the bearded man, a monstrous double-sided ax. At the same moment, Nyx stopped growling.

And then burst into flames.

Chapter 5

RESCUED, MAYBE

Zed and Tuesday stared, momentarily forgetting their intended escape. Nyx's soft brown eyes were now glowing the same electric shade of blue as the flames rippling and crackling along her back. Smoke and tiny blue embers wafted out of her mouth with each breath, her teeth glinting in the flickering light of her snarl.

It's difficult to say which Zed and Tuesday found more shocking: intruders with transforming weapons standing in their living room, or their house pet performing a bonfire impression. Beardy and Eyebrow Man, on the other hand, did not seem shocked at all. The bearded man lunged forward, swinging his ax, but Nyx dodged out of the way. The ax struck the floor and stuck fast. Nyx dove past him and sank her teeth into Eyebrow Man's leg. He howled in pain and swept his sword in Nyx's direction, but again she darted away. He clutched at his leg, which now bore both bite wounds and burns.

"Tuesday, come on!" Zed pleaded, tugging her arm again. This time, Tuesday allowed him to steer her, stumbling numbly along in his wake. Each step seemed to pound the reality of their situation further into her mind: this was not a dream, this was really happening, and they really needed to get out of there. Together they scrambled out the back door, through the yard, and into the woods beyond.

"Where are we even going?" Tuesday yelled.

"Dad said if there was ever an emergency, we should run to the Meeting Tree!" Zed shouted back.

"To meet HIM! In case of a fire or something!"

"Well there is a fire!"

"Mom and Dad aren't here! They're not going to meet us at the tree! And I don't think the dog spontaneously combusting is the type of fire Dad had in mind!"

Tuesday soon discovered the difficulty in attempting to run and yell at the same time, so she let the matter go. They ran in frantic silence, their minds reeling with the sheer impossibility of the last five minutes, until they finally reached the tree. The Meeting Tree, as their father had dubbed it, was an ancient, massive oak, which stood in a small clearing by itself, as though all the younger and smaller trees had stepped back to maintain a respectful distance. They rammed right into it, hands outstretched, like it was the safe base in a game of tag.

"Well, we made it, at least," Zed gasped. "You have any ideas?"

Tuesday leaned against the tree, doubled over to catch her breath. "We should go to Mrs. Alvarez's," she panted. "She'll call the police. Maybe she can drive us somewhere safe to wait."

Zed considered this. Although Mrs. Alvarez was their nearest neighbor, her house was on the other side of the patch of woods surrounding theirs. It would take a couple more minutes of running to reach it, and there was no telling whether the men had followed them—they might run right into them. On the other hand, there was no particular safety about the Meeting Tree; they had just gone there out of habit...

Zed didn't have a chance to decide whether Mrs. Alvarez or the police would even believe their story. The air around them was suddenly illuminated as though an enormous spotlight had switched on above them. Tuesday looked up, expecting to find the source of the light, but saw only tree branches. She and Zed squinted against the light, which quickly intensified until they could not see anything at all. The forest around them melted away into a blinding blur.

The last thing Zed saw, before he was forced to close his eyes entirely, was a low, dark blob moving toward them at frightening speed. There was a thud as something large hit him in the chest, and he toppled over backward into the crunchy carpet of leaves on the forest floor. Then, as quickly as it had come, the light dimmed until only the dappled sunlight filtering through the tree branches remained.

Zed opened one eye. Nyx was sitting on his chest. Nyx took this as her cue to begin slurping his face with her tongue. She was no longer on fire—just the same hairy, slobbery dog she had been when he arrived home from school this afternoon. Tuesday sat up next to him, rubbing her eyes. As relieved as Zed was to see that Nyx had escaped unharmed, and was not setting this shirt on fire, he wasn't anxious to hold all her weight on his chest any longer. He heaved her off and peered up into the tree branches to see if he could spot the source of the light. There was nothing there, but yet, something looked…different. He could have sworn the Meeting Tree was taller…and where was the treehouse?

Nyx seemed completely unconcerned by the sudden appearance, and disappearance, of the light. In fact, she acted like she'd forgotten the armed intruders entirely. She snuffled around in the fallen leaves, trailing a scent that had caught her interest, and was soon out of sight in the underbrush.

"What was THAT?" Tuesday shouted. "As if this day couldn't get any weirder!"

"Tuesday?" Zed quavered, "I think this day just got even weirder."

Zed pointed straight ahead—at someone that definitely hadn't been there before the light. A rather short, oddly-dressed man strode toward them. The greying, wiry hair peeking out from beneath his tasseled red hat was the same length as the bristly scruff sprouting from his chin. He wore a faded purple tunic over leather trousers, and boots so tall they nearly swallowed his knees. He carried a rumpled bundle of cloth draped over one arm; his other arm was stretched forward, palm out, the way one might approach a bull that was still deciding whether or not to charge.

"Now don't scamper off or nuthin'," the man called to them. "Those thugs can't get back through 'less I phase 'em in, which I don't intend on."

"Who are you?" Tuesday yelled. "How did you get here? Did you cause that light? She had hoped to sound menacing, but the words that escaped her mouth were rather squeakier than she intended.

"Most folks call me Scrimbley. I'm aimin' to help you, if you'll let me. And as for gettin' here, I think you're a bit misorientated. See, I was here the whole time. It's you what's moved."

A realization settled on Zed the way an anvil lands on a cartoon character—completely without warning. They were not standing under the Meeting Tree at all—not anymore, anyway. Somehow, when the column of light shone on them, they had been transported somewhere else. The man hadn't appeared in their patch of woods—they had appeared in his.

"I s'pose it is my doing, in a manner of sayin' so," the man continued. "See, those soldiers forced me to let 'em through to your place, and I guess they thought I was afeared enough to bring 'em back after they captured you, like they told me, but Scrimbley had the last laugh!" He removed something shiny from his pocket and waved it in his clutched fist.

"Soldiers? You mean those guys with the gnarly weapons? What do you know about that?" Tuesday's anger smothered her fear.

Scrimbley withered under her accusing glare. "Now hold your biscuits!" he stammered. "They'dve skewered me like a boiled parsnip if I hadn't done what they wanted! They have quite the bone to pick with your father and—"

"Wait, WHAT?" Tuesday interrupted. "You know our father? Those sword-wielding maniacs know our father? And you helped them try to kidnap us? WHAT'S GOING ON?"

Though Zed thought these were all perfectly reasonable questions, it was instantly clear Tuesday had pushed too far. Scrimbley's face dissolved into a grimace.

"I didn't sign up for none of this. I saved your lives, and that's enough to be gettin' on with." He shoved the bundled cloth he had been holding into Zed's arms. Zed untangled the bundle until two separate hooded cloaks emerged.

"Now you best put these on. If you don't cover those funny clothes of yours, you'll stick out like a dodo in a flock of ducks." Without another word, he turned on his heel and walked away.

"HEY, WHO ARE YOU CALLING A DODO?" Tuesday roared at Scrimbley's retreating figure. He made no sign that he'd heard her; he just kept walking.

He didn't make it far. Nyx burst out of the undergrowth and bolted straight for Scrimbley. He flailed toward the nearest tree and scrabbled at the bark, desperately trying to climb it, but the lowest branch was well out of reach.

"Are you mad?" he shouted over his shoulder at Tuesday and Zed. "Run, before the beast rips you to ribbons!"

"Beast?" asked Zed. "You mean Nyx? That's just our dog."

"Dog, my bunions! That's a Gabriel Hound, or I'm a gecko's grandmother!"

"Mister, if you think she's scary now, you should have seen her ten minutes ago," Zed quipped.

Nyx sniffed at Scrimbley's boots, then leaped up to lick his face. Scrimbley toppled over backward and lay still, his arms shielding his face. Nyx pranced back to Zed and Tuesday.

"Am I dead yet?" Scrimbley whispered after a moment. He peeked through his fingers, then sat up and wiped his face with his sleeve. His clothes were so grimy that this rendered his face dirtier rather than cleaning it.

"Are you really tellin' me you brought that beast here with you?" he asked after he'd removed enough dog drool from his face.

"We didn't bring her, she jumped into the light at the last second!" Tuesday retorted. "And we didn't go anywhere willingly—you did this!"

"At least Nyx trusts him," Zed remarked to Tuesday. "She certainly treated the last people she met differently."

"Well, I don't," Tuesday huffed. "He just admitted he helped those guys find us. And he isn't doing a great job explaining how we got here. We don't even know where 'here' is."

"Falinnheim," Scrimbley said as he stood and brushed himself off. "Welcome to Falinnheim."

Chapter 6

WELCOME TO FALINNHEIM

"Where, exactly, is 'Falinnheim'?" Tuesday pressed. "I've never heard of it. And when are you going to explain how a beam of light could move us somewhere else?"

"Just as soon as you explain how you got a demon hound for a pet," Scrimbley sniffed.

"She's not a demon!" Tuesday had not forgotten Nyx's uncharacteristically flammable behavior that afternoon, but she certainly wasn't about to let some oddly-dressed old goober get away with insulting her dog. Besides, Scrimbley hadn't been around when Nyx defended them; he didn't know there was anything unusual about her. He was probably just afraid of dogs.

"Nyx is our mom's pet," Zed explained. "She's had her for years, before we were born even."

"She'd be goin' on at least a dozen years then. Doin' a lot of running and jumping for such an old dog, wouldn't you say?"

Tuesday didn't have an answer to that, which annoyed her greatly.

"Your turn," she grumped at Scrimbley. "Where are we, and how did we get here?"

"This contraption," Scrimbley said. "Moves people from your world over here, and vice versa." He pulled the shiny lump he'd held earlier out of his pocket and flicked it open. It looked a lot like a compass, but with two sets of needles, and a row of tiny adjustment knobs.

"Wait, your world?" Tuesday interrupted. "What planet are we on?"

"Earth, a'course," Scrimbley replied. He frowned and scratched his head. "Well, it is Earth, but I s'pose it's not your Earth. Not really sure how to explain it. See, Fallinheim's in this extra pocket you can't really get to without this thing."

Zed's eyes lit up. "You mean like another dimension? Awesome!"

"Call it what you like," Scrimbley said. "Point is, you never heard of Falinnheim because folk on this side spent the last four hundred years makin' sure of it. I'm not even s'posed to have this thing, strictly speaking. The powers that be aren't too keen on sendin' folk back and forth anymore."

"So why did you?" Zed asked with a thoughtful frown. "Bring us here, I mean."

Scrimbley's voice sharpened. "Would you rather be back there with those thugs? No one asked me to interfere, and I'm still not convinced I shoulda done it after all! Don't kick the spoon that stirs the soup!"

"Why is he talking about soup?" Tuesday whispered to Zed out of the corner of her mouth.

"Like, you know, 'Don't bite the hand that feeds you,'" Zed whispered back. "I think he means we should be a bit more grateful. He did get us out of a tight spot."

"A spot he put us in in the first place," Tuesday mumbled.

Scrimbley heard her. "Whole thing's been nothin' but a heap of trouble!" he complained. "And I'm not makin' the mistake of gettin' even more tangled in this web than I already am! Now you put on those cloaks, head to the nearest village, and pretend you never met ol' Scrimbley."

"We're not going anywhere until you tell us what's going on!" Tuesday insisted.

Scrimbley crossed his arms. "I'm not lettin' a couple of children order me about, even if you are—"

At that moment Nyx spotted a squirrel climbing down from a tree directly behind Scrimbley. Her ears pricked up. Her entire body stiffened, every hair standing on end, eyes locked onto her target like laser-guided missiles. She stood, frozen, for the space of a breath, then launched forward in pursuit of her quarry, barging past Scrimbley and knocking him to his knees. The compass sailed out of his hand and landed on a large rock, splintering in half and sending springs and knobs flying.

Somehow, Scrimbley looked both horrified and relieved. "Well, those soldiers definitely aren't comin' back here now," he said. "And neither is no one else."

"But—that means we can't get home!" said Tuesday.

"How many times do I need to explain?" Scrimbley shouted. "Those soldiers back there do not mean to invite you to tea! Gettin' back to where they are is no kind of a plan! You should be delighted there's no way for them to find you. Now be off with you!"

And this time, with Nyx busy harassing the local wildlife, there was no one to stop Scrimbley from walking away.

There was nothing left to do but follow Nyx. They walked along a dusty path worn into the forest floor that wandered in roughly the same direction as Nyx had, pulling the cloaks over their clothes as they walked.

"Even if we are, what?" Zed wondered aloud.

"Huh?"

"Scrimbley said he wasn't going to let kids tell him what to do, 'even if you are,' and then he got interrupted."

"Who knows. Who cares! I didn't understand half of what that guy had to say, and I don't believe half of what I did understand."

"Even if we are…from the 'other' Earth?" Zed mused. "But why would that be a reason to listen to us?"

"Even if we are…here with a big slobbery dog?" Tuesday suggested. "He did seem pretty scared of Nyx. Besides, that's really what you want to talk about? Not the part where Nyx lights up like a Roman candle, then goes back to chasing squirrels like nothing happened? Not the part where big angry dudes—from Earth, only not really— are mad enough at Dad to try to kidnap us? And, by the way, why would Dad even know people from some other…"

"Dimension," Zed reminded her.

"Yeah, that."

"That's the question, isn't it?"

There was a long silence before Zed spoke again. "Do you think Mom and Dad are really on a business trip?"

"I don't know," Tuesday sighed. "I don't know about anything anymore."

Chapter 7

TIME IS MONEY

Tuesday and Zed followed the sounds of Nyx crashing through the underbrush ahead. As they walked, the forest gradually gave way to meadow, and then the meadow to fields, and finally to the outskirts of a village. They passed rows of homes built of dark timbers nestled into mounds of earth, leaving only the front door and a window or two visible, with grass growing over their pointed rooftops. It was as if the houses had been planted in the mounds and were just beginning to sprout, pushing their sod blankets aside.

The dirt road cutting through the village bustled with people dressed in much the same manner as Scrimbley had been. He was right, Zed noted—their clothes would have looked out of place. Their sneakers and the cuffs of their jeans stuck out below the cloaks, of course, but on the whole Zed was satisfied the cloaks helped them blend in much better than they otherwise would have. The fact that Nyx was still off tromping through the woods didn't hurt either—he suspected the villagers' opinion of their dog, had she been with them, might be similar to Scrimbley's.

The village had an unusual, mismatched quality to it. While most of the villagers walked, a few traveled standing on what appeared to be hovering sleds. At one home they passed, chickens pecked and scratched in the grassy patch outside their coop, completely ignoring a small robot rolling along on tank treads, gathering the eggs from their nests. At another, a knot of young children knelt in a circle playing a game that looked a lot like marbles, except the marbles changed direction to strike each other without being touched by the players. It was like a fairy tale and a science fiction movie had collided.

At the center of town they found a large square clearing that formed a market of covered stalls. They reminded Tuesday of lemonade stands, except they were tended by adults, not children, and rather than just lemonade, offered every kind of ware imaginable. Tuesday and Zed wandered through the market, necks craning to see all the strange things offered in each stall. There were household goods like pottery and blankets, fruits and vegetables, books, baked goods, jewelry, and shoes; but also, robots, hovering sleds, and shiny devices Zed and Tuesday couldn't even imagine the uses for, covered with buttons, knobs, and levers. Some of the signs advertising the booth's goods were simple, printed on wood or paper; others were engraved in metal plaques, or projected holographic images of salesmen reciting the shop's offerings on a loop. One stall was even manned by a hologram: "Kyvek's Repair Services." Its sign read, "Schedule an appointment with the holo-attendant for service at your home." A pale green light projected the image of a young man sitting patiently at the booth, fingers laced together, his posture unnaturally straight. He faded slowly in and out of focus as he scanned the area in front of the stall for potential customers.

They stopped at an unattended stall with a large sign overhead. "Farabi's Chemist Supply," it read, "Lotions and Potions, Bits and Bobs, Ingredients of All Sorts." Its shelves were crammed with bottles, jars, boxes, and canisters of all descriptions. Zed and Tuesday peered curiously at the labels.

"Eye of newt?" Tuesday gagged, pointing to a small green pot with a gold-colored lid. "Seriously?"

"Hmm…quicksilver," Zed read on another container. The reflective silver contents swirled in the vial like a melted mirror.

"Hey, look at this one," Tuesday remarked, drawing Zed's attention to a corked glass shaped like an old-fashioned milk bottle. "Butterfly milk?" she read incredulously. "Do you think they actually milk butterflies to get it?"

"Butterflies are insects," Zed pointed out. "They don't make milk."

"I knew that," Tuesday said, her ears reddening slightly. "Well, maybe it's what baby caterpillars drink then."

"Same problem."

"Oh. Right."

"Maybe it just means a liquid form of some ingredient," Zed suggested. "You know, like milk of magnesia, or almond milk."

"So that would mean…it's liquefied butterflies? Gross! Who would want a bottle of that?"

"Probably the same person who needs a jar of newt eyes," Zed laughed.

A man carrying a large wooden crate filled with more bottles appeared around the corner of the booth and stepped behind the counter.

"Be with you in a moment," he said. "Just need to restock." His wrinkled face was as deeply lined as the folds of the bright blue turban covering his head. He tugged at his long salt-and-pepper beard and stared at a deep, empty shelf behind the counter. He placed two jars on the shelf, switched them, took one down, and replaced it with a different bottle. Finally, he returned them all to the crate on the counter.

"I'm very sorry for the wait," he said at last. "I've got to shelve all these containers, but they always seem to end up in the wrong places."

"Wrong places?" Tuesday asked. "It's your store. Can't you just put them wherever you want?"

"Not if I want to stay in business, I can't!" He reached underneath the counter and pulled on a pair of shiny black gloves. "This," he said, picking up a tall, thin vial from the crate, "is quicksilver. Very useful for making metal alloys, but it's also poisonous. It can't be stored next to ingredients that are edible, or that will be rubbed into the skin or hair. So that rules out eye of newt and butterfly milk."

Tuesday tried not to think about why eye of newt might qualify as "edible."

The merchant slipped off the gloves and selected a squat round metal canister. He cradled it carefully in both hands. "Nitroglycerin. It can explode if dropped. One container doesn't have enough in it to be really dangerous, but I can't be losing all my stock to accidents. So, it shouldn't be stored on the front row, or ends of the shelf, where it might be accidentally knocked down."

He gently placed the canister back in the crate. Then he picked up a small wooden box and pulled off the lid, revealing a bunch of jagged black pebbles. They sparkled slightly as they caught the last rays of evening sunlight. "Lodestone," he explained. "Natural magnets. Found this batch at the site of a lightning strike. When the lightning hit them, their magnetic field was activated. The first compasses were made of lodestone. Anyway, the box is so short that I can't reach it behind the taller bottles."

Zed squinted upward like he was trying to inspect his own forehead. His lips scrunched over to one side of his face. After a few thoughtful humming noises, he asked, "Does lodestone react with quicksilver?"

The merchant raised his eyebrows. "No—what does that have to do with anything?"

"One sec." Zed bent down and used a stick to draw in the dirt. After a minute or two of sketching, scratching things out, and trying again, he stood back up.

"There," he said to the merchant, pointing to his dirt diagram. "If you arrange your jars in this order, it will work out better."

The man peered over the counter. Zed had written two rows of capital letters representing the different ingredients' places on the empty shelf.

"See," Zed continued, "nitroglycerin on the middle of the back row, so it won't fall off. Quicksilver on one side of the nitroglycerin—it's in a tall jar, so it needs to be at the back. Butterfly milk on the other side—it's also in a tall bottle, but it can't be near the quicksilver. Eye of newt in front of the butterfly milk, and the lodestone in front of the quicksilver."

The merchant stared at the shelf for a moment, then at the crate on the counter, and then turned back to Zed. "By Thor's thumbs, you're right!" he exclaimed. "Many thanks!"

He reached into the box of lodestone and pulled one out. "A gift for the problem solver," he said, handing the pebble to Zed. "Now, what can I get for you?"

"We were just looking," Tuesday replied. "We don't have any money anyway."

Zed thanked him for the stone and dropped it into the pocket of his cloak, then followed Tuesday back into the crowd.

<hr>

THE POTION PROBLEM
Recorded after the fact, for posterity
By Zed

THE INGREDIENTS
- Quicksilver: Tall glass vial, poisonous, can't touch edibles
- Butterfly Milk: Tall glass bottle. Edible?
- Eye of Newt: Small green pot. Edible? (ew.)
- Nitroglycerin: Short metal canister. Explosive, handle with care.
- Lodestone: Small wooden box. Magnetic.

THE SOLUTION

Q N B
  L E

"I hadn't thought about money," Zed whispered to Tuesday. His stomach growled.

"It's getting late," Tuesday said, scanning the market. "We need to find some dinner and place to sleep, and figure out where Nyx has run off to."

She motioned to Zed to follow her and made a beeline for a stall she had just noticed: "New Angkor Bakery." Tuesday marched up to the booth and addressed the tall, plump woman behind the counter. "One loaf of bread, please."

"That'll be sixteen minutes," the woman replied, sounding bored. She held her palm out to Tuesday.

"That's ok, we don't mind waiting a few minutes," Tuesday said.

The woman's eyebrows scrunched together. "The loaf costs sixteen minutes." She frowned. "Do you have the money or not? You two are much too young to remember the days of freebread."

"Sorry, we're…not from around here," Tuesday offered.

Well, that's the understatement of the century, thought Zed.

Tuesday continued, "So, how can we pay with time?"

"You from the Outlands or something?" the woman asked suspiciously. "I thought all of Falinnheim used the same currency." She pulled a handful of copper coins with holes through the middle out of her apron pocket. "Workers earn money according to the amount of time they work. The average laborer earns eight hours a day," she explained, holding up a large coin. "People with fancier jobs, professors and doctors and such, might be paid more like twenty hours for a day's work, but no one earns less than an hour coin for an hour of work."

"And freebread?" Tuesday prompted.

"Used to be that all bakeries offered their most basic loaf of bread for free, and the palace paid them back—said no one deserved to go hungry. But it wasn't just the poor that ate it—everyone did. It was a point of pride for a bakery to offer the best-tasting freebread. If folks liked the freebread, they were more likely to buy pastries and such there. But that stopped years ago…" her voice trailed off for a moment before she looked at Tuesday again. "So, since the palace won't repay me for my bread anymore, it costs sixteen minutes." She held up one of the smaller coins.

"We…don't actually have any money," Tuesday confessed.

The baker's eyebrows scrunched together again.

"But," Tuesday continued quickly, "How about a trade?"

"You want to barter?" the baker asked. "What have you got?"

Tuesday grabbed the rock out of Zed's pocket and slapped it down on the counter. "Lodestone," she said. "It's magnetic, lightweight, and sparkly to boot. Surely that must be worth sixteen minutes."

The baker picked the stone up and rolled it between her fingers. Then she pulled a pin out of her hair and touched it to the stone. It stuck.

"I suppose it would be nice to have a place to keep extra hairpins," she agreed. She slipped the rock into her apron pocket and handed Tuesday a loaf of bread.

"Pleasure doing business with you," Tuesday replied. She shook the woman's hand and turned back into the crowd.

"Wow, that was really impressive!" said Zed. "I wouldn't have thought of that."

Tuesday smiled as she tore off a hunk of bread and handed it to her brother. "You're not the only problem solver around here."

FALINNHEIM'S CURRENCY

Recorded after the fact, for posterity, by Zed

- Coins = Hours (Copper, center holes conserve metal and allow stringing onto rings for security)
- Minimum wage: 1 hour of work = 1 Hour coin (Sounds fair. Keeps inflation in check? Easier to know if a purchase is overpriced)
- Average daily salary = 8 hours (time) = 8 Hours (coins)
- Average yearly salary = 8 hours/day X 5 days/week = 40 hours/week

= 40 hours/week X 52 weeks/year = 2080 hours/year

= 2080 hours/year - vacation and sick days (2 weeks?)

= approx. 2000 Hours per year

Chapter 8

A SONG OF SIXPENCE

The next order of business was to locate Nyx. And as it turned out, she was very easy to find. All they had to do was follow the screaming.

"Quick, hide!" urged a man in a crimson cloak as they made their way to the edge of the market square. "There's a Gabriel Hound loose in the village!"

"Oh good, which way?" Zed asked. The man stared at Zed like he had two heads but pointed him in the direction of a side street echoing with panicked noises. Zed and Tuesday waded through the tide of fleeing villagers until the street emptied. Nyx darted around a corner, spotted them, and bounded up carrying a mangled mass of feathers in her mouth. She dropped the dead bird at Tuesday's feet and bowed playfully, waiting for Tuesday to throw it for her to fetch.

"Ugh! Nyx!" Tuesday grimaced. "I'm not touching that!"

"I think we'd better stay off the street until things calm down," Zed suggested. Nyx scooped up the bird and trotted along after Zed and Tuesday with her prize. They continued down a narrow alley until they noticed a cellar door propped open behind a building.

Nyx stepped down the cellar stairs and settled herself in one corner of the dark, low-ceilinged room. She arranged the bird between her paws and began to pluck off feathers one by one, just as daintily as if she'd been at a tea party.

"After you," Tuesday said, and followed Zed into the cellar, closing the door behind them.

It was a long night. They had their cloaks for blankets and used some grain sacks they found as pillows, but the cellar was dirty and uncomfortable. Also, very boring. There was no light, nothing to do; they were left alone in the darkness with their thoughts, which bobbed through their heads like debris from a shipwreck churning in the waves of a dark and unforgiving ocean.

Tuesday awoke the next morning to a crick in her neck and Nyx's cold nose in her ear. Her eyes creaked open. Nyx licked her face and bounded over to the cellar stairs, looking back over her shoulder expectantly. Pale slivers of early morning sunlight peeked between the slats of the door.

Zed and Tuesday shared the remains of yesterday's bread as they wandered the village streets. Nyx ran off into the woods again, which was just as well considering the alarm her presence had caused the previous evening. They found the market stalls had all been removed from the town's square, leaving only a deserted, dusty clearing peppered with footprints.

The shoppers' absence revealed something Zed and Tuesday had not noticed before: at one edge of the clearing stood the village well. A stone chute with a pulley and bucket, Zed thought, would have matched their surroundings best—like a wishing well from a fairy tale. This one, however, looked much more futuristic: a gleaming white pillar, about the same height as Tuesday, with a smooth depression in one side, presumably to place a bucket or pitcher in to catch the water. Zed turned a lever just beneath this cavity, and as he suspected, cold, clear water flowed out from the ceiling of the indentation.

"It's just like the water dispenser in the door of our fridge back home," Zed observed. "Only, you know, huge." They had to cup the water in their hands to drink, as they had no other container to catch it in, but this gave them an opportunity to wash off their hands and faces.

"Yick. What I wouldn't give for a toothbrush!" Tuesday complained. "My teeth feel like they're wearing fuzzy slippers!"

"Hey, look at this," Zed called. He walked over to investigate a large, freestanding slab of wood a stone's throw away from the well. Large letters carved into the top read "New Angkor Community Bulletin." Both sides of the board were littered with papers tacked haphazardly over the surface: help wanted ads, sales flyers, invitations to public events. Prominently displayed in the center was a map of the village.

"So, we're here, by the well," said Zed, jabbing a finger at the map. "We saw the market square already. The forest where we met Scrimbley yesterday is to the west. There are roads leading to other towns to the north, east, and southeast."

"You act like we're headed somewhere particular," Tuesday said as she glanced over the papers on the opposite side of the board. "What does it matter where we are? We don't have any way of getting home."

"Not yet, but we'll figure something out. Any of those flyers advertising illicit inter-dimensional travel?" Zed joked.

"No, Tuesday sighed. "Sure are a lot of missing person reports though."

Zed came over to her side of the board. While a few of the pages had headlines like "Fresh Eggs, Eighteen Minutes a Dozen," and "Chess Tournament this Saturday," many more said things like MISSING—PLEASE HELP and HAVE YOU SEEN ME? There were also wanted posters for criminals; petty thieves, mostly, although one offered a reward of two thousand hours for the capture of someone called the Green Fly.

"Hmm," Tuesday said. "This is weird. Why would someone post a nursery rhyme here?" She tore the top sheet off of a stack of identical papers and handed it to Zed.

He read the page:

KEEP A SONG OF SIXPENCE, A POCKET
   FULL OF RYE,
FOUR AND TWENTY BLACKBIRDS
   HIDDEN IN A PIE.
WHEN THE PIE WAS OPENED, THE BIRDS
   BEGAN TO SING;
WASN'T THAT A DAINTY DISH TO SET
   BEFORE THE KING?

"Yeah, that is strange," Zed admitted. He read the lines over once more. "Something doesn't seem right about this, though."

"Like what?"

"I'm not sure. I think it might be written wrong."

"What do you mean, wrong?" Tuesday asked. "It rhymes and everything. I remember reading a book, when I was little, that had an illustration of all the little birds poking their heads out of the pie crust to sing. Although I never could understand why anyone would bake live birds into a pie…"

"That's it!" Zed exclaimed. "The birds weren't 'hidden' in the pie, they were 'baked' in!"

"So they got one word wrong, who cares?"

Zed folded the paper and stuffed it in the pocket of his cloak. "I need more time to think about it. I'll figure it out."

After some discussion, they decided to take the road heading north. They couldn't risk Nyx drawing any more attention—better to start fresh in some other village. They walked all morning, passing groves of tall, soldier-straight pines, sweeping firs, and graceful white-barked trees that looked something like birches, except where the trees at home were just beginning to put on their autumn wardrobes of red and gold, these leaves seemed to be turning dark blue. Sometimes Nyx trotted alongside them, and sometimes she veered off the path to investigate a rustle in the bushes or follow an interesting scent. They weren't too worried about keeping track of her though; there was no point in trying. She never listened to anyone but Mom anyway. And besides, Nyx had already proven she was more than capable of handling any situation that might come up.

"I just thought of something," said Zed, mostly to himself, as they walked along. "Those guys that attacked us yesterday…" Had it really only been yesterday? "Scrimbley called them soldiers."

"Yeah. So?"

"If they're soldiers, that means they have a job to do. Someone pays them to enforce laws, or find criminals, or protect villages, or something."

"I guess…"

"So that means there are more of them. Even if those two particular guys can't get back here, there might be others looking for us."

Tuesday let that news sink in. It was not an encouraging thought.

"Scrimbley also said he wasn't supposed to have that compass thingy!" she argued. "Why would soldiers force him to use it, instead of just arresting him?"

"Good point," Zed admitted. "Their beef with Dad sounded kind of personal. Maybe if they weren't acting on official business, they didn't tell anyone else what they were up to."

"But we don't know that for sure."

"No. We don't," he agreed. "And that brings up another point."

"What's that?" asked Tuesday. She was beginning to wish Zed didn't think so much.

"The soldiers did something they knew was illegal. That means we can't trust them."

Tuesday rolled her eyes. She didn't need anyone to tell her that big guys breaking into her house with shape-shifting weapons were people to avoid, but Zed sort of had a point. She was used to viewing police officers, the military, and other government officials with trust and respect. The realization that the officials of Falinnheim were bad guys (at least two of them, anyway) was unnerving.

They spotted a sign by the side of the road with an arrow pointing in the direction they had come from: "New Angkor, 4 Leagues." Below it was an arrow pointing in the direction they were heading, marked "Persepolis, 2 Leagues."

"I thought a league measured depth, not distance," Zed said with a frown. "Like Twenty Thousand Leagues Under the Sea."

"Well, however far it is, it's half as far to the next village as we've traveled already," Tuesday reasoned. She looked straight up and squinted into the clouds. "The sun is overhead, so it's got to be nearly noon now. We started walking right after breakfast, and we've come four leagues in that time, so I'd say a league takes about an hour to walk."

"Speaking of noon, I'm starving," said Zed. "I wish we had more of that bread."

Nyx came crashing through the undergrowth to their left, crossed the path, and continued through the woods to their right, out of sight again. After a moment they heard splashing noises. They left the road and followed her through the trees, over a large boulder, and down a gully until they caught up with her, lapping up water from a stream.

"Look!" Tuesday pointed across the stream. On the opposite bank was a bramble of raspberry bushes, drooping under the weight of the ripe fruit.

They picked all the berries they could carry, holding up the corners of their cloaks to form a sling to drop them in, then settled on some rocks by the stream to eat. Zed pulled the nursery rhyme paper out of his pocket, smoothed out the folded creases against his leg, and reread it, absentmindedly popping berries into his mouth.

"So the word 'hidden' was used in place of 'baked'. That could be a simple mistake, I guess. The lines all rhyme, so the words at the ends of the lines are probably correct: rye, pie, sing, king…"

"Sing!" Tuesday exclaimed. "The title of the nursery rhyme is 'Sing a Song of Sixpence.' But it isn't written that way here!" She pointed to the first line. "It says 'Keep a Song of Sixpence!' Which doesn't make any sense anyway—I'm not sure why I didn't notice that sooner…"

"So they changed the words 'sing' and 'baked'. Hmm… I have no idea what that means." Zed ran his fingers through his hair. "And why post this in the first place, anyway? If it was on the bulletin board, whoever put it there must have wanted someone else to see it…"

"Maybe it's some kind of secret message!" said Tuesday.

"Seriously, Tuesday, will you quit it with the conspiracy theories?" Zed moaned. "You're always coming up with wild ideas about—"

Zed stopped. He stared at the page like his eyes might pop out of his head.

"Woah. Tuesday," he whispered. "You're right. You're actually right." He pointed to the page. "It's not what the rhyme ought to say that's important—it's what was changed."

He traced his finger around the two "wrong" words in the rhyme: KEEP and HIDDEN.

"'Keep hidden.' I wonder who the message was for?" said Tuesday.

Just then, Nyx's ears perked up. She froze in place, staring over the ridge of the gully toward the forest road. Tuesday put a finger to her lips. She and Zed crept toward the ridge and peeked over.

Two women glided over the road on hover sleds, in the same direction Zed and Tuesday had been traveling.

"Did you hear about the commotion at the market last night?" one woman asked. "They say a Gabriel Hound was spotted in the village square!"

"Honestly, Hilda, you'll believe anything!" the other woman cackled. "No one's seen a Gabriel Hound in these parts since Osiris the Merciless died."

"Well old Arvid, the weaver, told me his neighbor Asura heard from her son Naman that two children were seen running from the New Angkor market around sundown, and the—"

The women sped out of earshot, but Zed and Tuesday didn't need to hear any more.

"Whoever that message was for," said Tuesday grimly, "it's not bad advice."

Chapter 9

JACK AND JILL

They decided it was best to stay off the road from now on and follow the river instead. It ran in the same direction as the road but was far enough into the woods that they wouldn't be noticed by any other travelers that came along.

It was another two hours, just as Tuesday had predicted, before they arrived at the outskirts of the next town. "Town" wasn't really the right word for it though, Zed decided. New Angkor had been a town—this was a city. All the roads they had traveled on so far had been dirt paths, but the roads of Persepolis were paved with vast slabs of smooth black stone.

Zed, Tuesday, and Nyx crouched at the edge of the woods, concealed behind a boulder, and monitored the entrance to the city. Two identical statues of griffins carved from the same stone as the road stood guard, one on each side of the road. Each had one wing raised, with their carved feathers meeting in the middle to form an archway. Dozens of people milled about, entering and leaving the city; some traveled on foot, some on hover sleds, but they were all absorbed in their own concerns—none paid any attention to their audience in the forest.

"You and Nyx go wait by the river," Tuesday whispered as she darted out from behind the boulder.

"What are you doing?" Zed hissed in alarm.

"I just want to check things out. I'll be back before you know it."

Without a backward glance, she strolled onto the road, through the archway, and disappeared into the crowd.

Zed draped an arm around the dog's neck to keep her from following Tuesday.

"You know, Nyx," Zed murmured, "I can't help but admire her confidence, but sometimes I wish she'd take a moment to look before she leaps."

While Zed and Nyx tromped through the trees back to the banks of the river, Tuesday weaved her way through the city's streets. Persepolis could not have been more different from New Angkor's turf houses and quaint market square. The sleek stone walkways were surrounded by equally polished buildings of stone and metal and glass, apartment buildings and offices and shops, all bustling with activity. Some of the shops had holograms, as in New Angkor, but these were stationed on the sidewalks by the shop entrances, welcoming customers like flickering butlers.

As Tuesday passed a hologram in front of a barber shop, the pale green image of a bald man with an elaborately curled handlebar mustache turned to address her.

"What a lovely afternoon, madam!" it said, beaming. "Can I interest you in a trim? Only two hours!"

Tuesday was not convinced the hologram could do more than recite a few programmed phrases, but she answered it anyway. "No thanks. Unless you know some way for me to get home, I don't think there's much you can help me with."

The hologram maintained its chipper grin but gazed blankly out at the crowd instead of facing Tuesday. Just as Tuesday was about to continue on her way, it spoke. She turned around in surprise; the man's lips did not move, and the voice sounded slightly different than before, but the words were definitely coming from the direction of the hologram: "Jack and Jill work up the hill to fetch a pail together. Jack fell down and broke his crown, and Jill came tumbling after."

"What did you say?" Tuesday gasped. "Were you talking to me?"

The man did not answer. His vacant expression and plastered-on smile remained motionless. Tuesday held her breath, waiting to see if the hologram would do something else. Finally, it turned back to face her.

"What a lovely afternoon, madam! Can I interest you in a trim? Only two hours!" it repeated.

Tuesday raced down the sidewalk to another shop with a hologram out front. The green, flickering image of a young woman with her hair in long ringlets chirped, "Welcome to Xerxes, the finest restaurant in all of Persepolis! Our specials today are jeweled rice, lamb kebabs with pomegranate sauce, and—"

"Can you help me get home?" Tuesday interrupted.

The woman stared blankly ahead, but just as before, a man's voice chanted, "Jack and Jill work up the hill to fetch a pail together. Jack fell down and broke his crown, and Jill came tumbling after."

"What does that mean?" Tuesday demanded. "Who is that message for?"

"Welcome to Xerxes, the—"

Tuesday ran to the next hologram, several shops down. The image of a man built like a refrigerator folded his arms menacingly at the entrance to an apartment building.

"No one enters without invitation from a resident," he rumbled. "Who do you wish to—"

Tuesday didn't wait to hear any more. "I need help getting home!"

The doorman did not respond, but the same voice as before repeated the rhyme.

"Zed needs to hear about this," Tuesday decided aloud. Calmly this time, to avoid alarming passers-by, she made her way back to the griffin gate.

Chapter 10

THE TROUBLE WITH FISH

"Wait, say it again," Zed instructed. He grabbed a stick and copied the rhyme in the dirt as Tuesday dictated it. "Are you sure you remember every word exactly?"

"I ought to, I heard it over and over," said Tuesday. "Their lips never moved, and it was a different voice than the holograms used. This was definitely not part of their regular programming. It only happened in response to the words 'home' and 'help.'"

"I'd really like to see these holograms myself, but we can't go together, or Nyx will follow us, and she definitely won't go unnoticed."

"I can stay with her while you take a turn," Tuesday offered. "What did you two do while I was gone?"

Zed pointed to a group of round rocks, each about the size of a softball, arranged in a circle a short distance from the river.

"I pulled some rocks from the stream and found some dry twigs and branches in the woods—I was planning to make a campfire, but then I realized I don't have any way to light it. I tried scraping rocks together to make sparks, but I couldn't get the twigs to light."

"We'll work on that later," Tuesday said. "Right now, I'm starving! We need to figure out something to eat."

"Well, we don't have anything left to barter with in town. And I don't see any berry bushes…" Zed sat down on a boulder and gazed absentmindedly into the river as he tried to come up with something. "I guess we could try fishing," he said at last.

Tuesday set to work making a fishing pole. She found a long stick and was searching for a vine to use as a line when she realized she didn't have anything to use for a hook. Or bait. A net was her next idea, which would have worked beautifully, if she had actually found any vines to make it from. But she didn't. In the end, she removed her socks and shoes, cuffed her jeans, and waded into the stream, determined to catch a fish with her bare hands.

After nearly an hour of stumbling over rocks and being outsmarted by fish, Tuesday stomped out of the stream and pulled socks back over her wet, cold, numb feet. "This is impossible!" she complained.

She turned back toward the water. "Why do you have to be so slippery?" she yelled at the fish. "Just let me eat you!"

Nyx waded into the middle of the stream, then stood still. Her eyes glowed blue, as they had the previous afternoon, but just for an instant. As they dissolved back to their usual brown, half a dozen lifeless fish floated to the surface. She snatched the nearest one in her mouth and splashed back onto the bank.

Zed dashed into the water, shoes and all, to grab the remaining fish before they floated downstream.

"Nyx! What on earth did you do?" Tuesday exclaimed. "And whatever it was, why didn't you do it an hour ago?"

"It looked like the fish were shocked. I think she must have sent an electric pulse into the water," Zed concluded.

"Unbelievable," said Tuesday. "She spends more than a decade as a completely normal, boring house pet, and now out of nowhere she wants to show off a bunch of party tricks."

"Well, to be honest, it's been a rather unusual couple of days. She didn't really have a reason to do any of this until now."

"I don't suppose you could light the fire for us, too?" Tuesday suggested to Nyx, who was enjoying her fish.

Nyx cocked her head to one side.

Tuesday grabbed two stones and scraped them together over Zed's pile of twigs. "You know, fire? Warm, bright, turns slimy raw fish into something edible?"

Nyx trotted over to the circle of stones. Tuesday scrambled backwards, thinking the dog might erupt into flames, but instead Nyx snorted a puff of smoke out of her nose over the wood. A few tiny blue embers floated down and landed in the twigs. The sparks glowed, the twigs smoked, then finally they lit.

The first streaks of orange were just beginning to creep onto the horizon by the time they finished their dinner. They were still alone in the woods with no way to get home, but it didn't seem to matter so much at the moment. It was much easier to feel hopeful with full stomachs and dry socks.

While Nyx stretched out in front of the fire licking her paws clean, Zed pulled the folded paper out of his cloak pocket. He turned it over to the blank side and used the burnt end of a stick to scribble the holograms' message in soot:

JACK AND JILL WORK UP THE HILL
TO FETCH A PAIL TOGETHER.
JACK FELL DOWN AND BROKE HIS
   CROWN,
AND JILL CAME TUMBLING AFTER.

"Now that we know the pattern, breaking the code should be easy," he told Tuesday. "All we have to do is remember how the rhyme is supposed to go."

Tuesday read the page over Zed's shoulder. "Well, I know for sure the rhyme said they were fetching a pail 'of water,'" she said. "So that's one change—'together.'"

"I think there's something different about the first line too, but I can't remember how that part of the rhyme goes. 'Jack and Jill walked up the hill', or maybe 'went up the hill...'"

"Walked, went, something like that. Doesn't matter. The point is, the word has been changed." Tuesday took the paper from Zed and read it again. "I think the rest is right. So that gives us the message: WORK TOGETHER."

"That's good advice I guess, but it's not very specific." Zed frowned. "Someone went to a lot of trouble to hack into the holograms' programming. I wonder who these messages are for?" Zed stared into the fire, lost in thought. "I need to see this for myself," he determined at last.

"It's sunset already—you only have half an hour or so before it gets dark," Tuesday warned.

"No problem," he assured her. "I just want to take a quick look around; I'll be back in no time."

Chapter 11

HEY DIDDLE DIDDLE

The first hologram Zed stumbled across was of a tall, thin, elderly man. The man's protruding cheekbones and slicked-back white hair reminded Zed of a skull. The light of the projection actually made his hair look a bit green, though, Zed decided—more like a moldy skull.

The man sneered down at Zed approaching the ornate columns of the building's entrance. "The Persepolis city offices are closed," the hologram said. "They are open between noon and two on alternating Thursdays. Though children," he added, as though the word tasted bitter on his tongue, "have no business here at any time."

Zed ignored this—it was just a hologram, after all.

"What's your favorite color?" Zed asked.

The man clasped his hands behind his back and gazed into the distance.

Zed tried again. "Do you know how to get back to

the other dimension?"

No response.

"I need help getting home," he said at last.

The man did not move, but a voice repeated the rhyme, just as Tuesday had said.

Satisfied with his experiment, Zed continued on toward the city center. There was no market square or bulletin board, as in New Angkor, but he did find a large fountain set in the middle of an unusually wide street. An enormous statue of a man holding a staff stood in the center; six smaller figures knelt in a circle around him, pouring water out of large vases into the pool at the base of the fountain. A plaque at the man's feet read, "THE LIBERATOR."

Zed sat on the fountain's ledge and looked around. He saw couples strolling arm in arm, large hover sleds delivering crates of supplies to stores, a father helping a toddler step over a curb. He surveyed the shops surrounding the fountain for any other holograms and spotted one outside a grocery. A young man with a red beard and an old woman stepped out the door carrying cloth sacks filled to the brim with their shopping.

"Shall I summon a clerk to carry your bags?" asked the flickering image of a freckly teenage boy dressed in an apron.

"No, thank you," the woman replied. "My son will help me take them home."

The hologram faced the street with a blank stare. The shoppers continued on their way, but then turned back to the hologram in surprise as a different voice began chanting, "Jack and Jill work up the hill to fetch a—"

"What's that supposed to mean?" the woman asked her son over the sound of the voice still prattling on.

"No idea," he said. "Must be a programming glitch or something."

THE HOLOGRAMS' RIDDLE
Dictated to Zed, by Tuesday, at Zed's insistence
Recorded after the fact, for posterity

STATEMENTS TO HOLOGRAMS
- "No thanks. Unless you know some way for me to get home, I don't think there's much you can help me with" (Response: Riddle, see below)
- "What did you say? Were you talking to me?" (Response: none)
- "Can you help me get home?" (Response: Riddle, see below)
- "What does that mean? Who is that message for?" (Response: sales pitch)
- "I need help getting home." (Response: Riddle, see below)
- "What's your favorite color?" (Response: none)
- "Do you know how to get back to the other dimension?" (Response: none)

- "I need help getting home." (Response: Riddle, see below)
- "No thanks, my son will help me take them home." (Response: Riddle, see below)

THE RIDDLE
"Jack and Jill work up the hill to fetch a pail together. Jack fell down and broke his crown, and Jill came tumbling after."

CONCLUSION
Common elements of statements that resulted in Riddle: "Home", "Help". Statement intent and content were irrelevant.

Zed sat by the fountain, immersed in his own thoughts, enjoying the soft breeze ruffling his hair. He felt something brush against his leg and looked down. The wind was blowing some littered flyers across the street; one of the papers had plastered itself flat against his shin. He picked it up, expecting to see a sales advertisement.

It wasn't.

HEY, DIDDLE THE DIDDLE,
THE CAT AND THE FIDDLE,
THE DOG JUMPED OVER THE MOON.
THE LITTLE DOG KNOWS TO SEE SUCH
  SPORT,
AND THE DISH RAN AWAY WITH THE SPOON.

Zed stuffed the paper in his pocket.

On his way back to camp, Zed passed a small gathering outside a bookstore. Each of the people congregated at the entrance held a paper. Snatches of their conversation floated past as Zed neared the store.

"—could be some kind of advertisement—"

"Isn't 'The Cat and the Fiddle' that new tavern on Babylon Street?"

"No, that's 'The Fat Fiddle.'"

"Yeah, I ate lunch there last week. The artichoke appetizer was all right, but—"

Zed approached the store and pulled the flyer out of his pocket. "I found one of those too," he mentioned to a woman at the edge of the group.

"They're all over town!" she replied. "Any idea what it is?"

"You mean you've never heard it before?" Zed asked, puzzled.

"No, should I have?"

"It's a nursery rhyme," Zed explained. "Young children memorize them. You know, like 'Mary Had a Little Lamb', 'Little Miss Muffet', 'Humpty Dumpty…'"

"Humpty Dumpty?" the man next to her scoffed. "What's that rhyme about, a camel?"

"Really?" Zed prodded. "You've never heard of Old King Cole? Peter Pumpkin Eater? Jack and Jill?"

"Jack and Jill…aren't they that singing duo from Olympus Minor?"

Another man chimed in. "You know, this reminds me of a sign I saw this morning at the crossroads on the north side of town—it had a weird rhyme. Couldn't make head nor tail of it…something about sheep."

Zed wanted to ask the man more about this sign, but he never got the chance. As the man happened to glance over Zed's shoulder, his face froze. "Soldiers!" he hissed.

The crowd instantly dispersed. Some people walked down the street and ducked into other shops. Some took the alleys between shops. One man even hid in the bushes under the bookstore's window. Zed, having no other ideas, entered the bookstore, skirted up a row of shelves, and selected a book at random. He kept one eye on the door as he buried his nose in the pages and tried to look thoroughly interested in Soaps, Salves, and Soups: 200 Uses for Seaweed.

A large, lumpy looking man and a shorter woman, her blonde hair caught back in a tight braid, entered the store. They were identically dressed in orange tunics covered with protective vests made of rows of black circles overlapping like scales. Each bore a silver shoulder badge engraved with a figure of a wolf.

"Your payment's overdue," the man barked at the clerk trembling behind the counter.

"Please!" the clerk begged. "I already paid you this month! I won't be able to stay in business if I give you any more!"

"That was last month," argued the woman. "And your shop definitely won't stay in business if we don't protect it." She pulled a polished metal cylinder out of a loop at the side of her vest. As she pointed it to the clerk's chest, it morphed into a large hammer.

"It would be a shame if you arrived at work one morning to discover all your windows had been shattered," she continued. The hammer stretched itself into a dagger, brushing the clerk's apron. "Or if you met bandits in the alley on your way home." The soldier stroked the blade of the dagger thoughtfully, almost lovingly, before it melted back into the cylinder shape she had started with. She tucked it back into the side of her armored vest.

The clerk scowled as he handed over a small bag of coins. "Someday the Liberator will discover your treachery! He'll throw you all in prison!"

"Tyrren wants his villages and cities kept in order," she laughed. "And they are. I don't think he's terribly particular as to how.

"Come on Baldur," she said, turning to her partner. "We have other rounds to make." He laughed as the bag clinked in his grip.

Zed stayed in the shop long after they'd left, his face still hidden in the book. He didn't learn a single thing about seaweed, but he had plenty to discuss with Tuesday.

Where to start? Zed made it back to their camp right at dusk, but when Tuesday asked for a report on his excursion, there was so much to tell he was afraid he'd leave something out. He took a seat by the fire and recounted his experiment with the hologram, the new rhyme, and the fact that no one else in town seemed to be familiar with nursery rhymes.

"What was it Scrimbley said? About his compass thingy?" Tuesday rubbed her temples with her fingertips as though trying to pluck out the memory by hand.

"What's Scrimbley got to do with anything?" Zed asked.

"He said something about travel between dimensions being illegal...that people on this side wanted to make sure no one found out about Falinnheim."

"Pretty sure he said it wasn't legal anymore, but it used to be. Five hundred years ago, or so?"

"Four hundred!" Tuesday remembered. "So, the last time Falinnheim had much contact with our world was more than four hundred years ago!"

"And?" Zed coaxed.

"And I bet nursery rhymes, or at least the ones we're familiar with, are newer than that!"

"That would explain why no one else seemed to recognize them," Zed agreed. "But that would mean…"

"I know." Tuesday nodded. "The code only works if you already know the rhymes. So, whoever sent the messages must be from our world. And whoever they're for is too."

Zed pulled the latest page out of his pocket. By now, they were so familiar with the code that it wasn't even necessary to talk through it, as they had before. Tuesday held the paper before the fire, her eyes dancing over the lines, reading and rereading in disbelief.

THE DOG KNOWS.

Was it possible? Tuesday and Zed slowly turned to stare at Nyx. She was busy contorting herself into a hairy pretzel, scratching her ear with her back paw. Then she spotted her tail and hobbled about in a circle, chasing it. After three or four revolutions, she caught it; the tuft of fur sticking out of the side of her mouth wagged feebly.

"No," Zed whispered. "It couldn't be…"

"Knows what?" Tuesday wondered aloud.

No matter how they tried to avoid it, there was only one rational conclusion: the messages were for them. But that conclusion raised an even more important question: who were they from?

It was well past nightfall, and he and Tuesday were already curled beneath their cloaks next to the fire, before Zed remembered he had left one very important element out of his account on Persepolis. Soldiers.

"And you're sure they didn't see you? Or mention anything about looking for two kids, or a Gabriel Hound?" Tuesday asked when Zed finished his tale.

"I'm sure! But just because they didn't mention it to the clerk doesn't mean they aren't looking for us."

"Maybe we ought to take turns keeping watch," Tuesday suggested. "Someone might see the fire and come investigate. And besides, who knows what kind of wild animals might be stalking around in the dark out here."

"Don't worry," Zed assured her. "We've got Nyx with us, and she's definitely scarier than anything we might run into tonight. Including soldiers."

Tuesday wasn't so sure about that, but it didn't matter. Struggling to keep her eyes open after a long day of walking was a losing battle.

Chapter 12

LITTLE BO PEEP

Leftover smoked fish was not Tuesday's idea of a delicious breakfast. In fact, she would even have preferred dry Bran Brix. But fish was all they had. An unexpected camping trip in another dimension is no time to be picky, Tuesday told herself. She resolved to eat a heaping stack of warm, fluffy pancakes as soon as she got home.

A chilly mist still hung in the air, and the sun was not yet truly awake, when they finished eating and prepared for the day's journey. Breaking camp took a matter of seconds; Zed simply kicked some dirt over the remains of their now-extinguished fire while they pulled on their cloaks.

They picked their way through the trees, following the river around the city rather than through it. It took a bit longer, but the direct route through Persepolis wasn't an option with Nyx trotting along beside them.

"Where did you say we're heading?" Tuesday asked.

"Someone at the bookstore told me there are crossroads on the opposite side of the city," Zed explained. "I think there might be another message there."

They only had to walk twenty minutes or so before they spied the main road again. The northern entrance to the city was similar to the southern gate, but instead of griffins, the road was flanked with statues of a creature Zed and Tuesday had never seen before. The gigantic stone figures resembled bulls, but with only one horn, set in the middle of the forehead. Although they had hairy manes and tufted tails, their legs seemed to be covered in scales. The statues faced each other, their horns crossing to form a peak over the road. The area was deserted; while Zed imagined a few early risers inside the city were beginning to filter into the streets, they could see no one.

"Those have got to be the world's ugliest unicorns," Zed remarked as he stared at the statues.

"Which world?" Tuesday added.

Zed shrugged. "Either one. Falinnheim or Earth. Or whatever people here would call where we come from."

A few yards in front of the gate stood a tall metal pole with three arrows protruding from it, each pointing the way down a different dirt path that forked off from the main road. Each arrow was engraved with the name of the city or village it led to: Etrusia to the left, Kyoto to the right, and Alexandria straight ahead.

"Okay," Tuesday said, "Here's your crossroads. So, where's this message you heard about?"

Zed walked up to the pole and looked around. Forest lay to either side, but in the center, next to the road leading to Alexandria, was a grassy clearing. A small wooden sign was staked into the field, with painted-on sheep grazing around a block of text in the middle:

LITTLE BO PEEP HAS LOST HER SHEEP
AND DOESN'T KNOW WHERE TO
  FOLLOW THEM.
LEAVE THEM ALONE, AND THEY'LL
  COME HOME
WAGGING THE DOG BEHIND THEM.

Tuesday followed Zed up to the sign. Zed watched her face as she read. "Are you seeing the same message I am?" he asked when she'd finished.

Tuesday nodded.

FOLLOW THE DOG.

The previous evening's excitement at working out the new messages evaporated like a half-forgotten dream. Doubt seeped in. Yesterday, she and Zed were convinced these messages had to be meant for them, but now Tuesday found the idea nearly impossible to swallow. After all, who even knew they were there? If Scrimbley had anything to tell them, he could have done it in person. And even if she could suspend disbelief long enough to accept that the messages were directed at them, the content was problematic. "Keep Hidden" and "Work Together" were harmless enough, but how could they possibly trust all their decision-making to a dog? What did she know? And if they followed her, where would she lead them?

Tuesday looked down at the dog sitting patiently beside her. Nyx returned her gaze and wagged her tail. "I can't believe I'm saying this, but...Nyx, which way should we go?"

Immediately, Nyx stood and walked over to the sign. She sniffed at the base of the stake for a moment, then trotted down the path to the right. She stopped after a few yards and looked back over her shoulder at Zed and Tuesday.

"Kyoto it is," Zed declared. "I sure hope you know what you're doing, Nyx."

Chapter 13

AN UNFORTUNATE MEETING

The road to Kyoto was nearly indistinguishable, at first, from the path they had followed the previous morning out of New Angkor: a wide dirt trail surrounded by forest. Birds chirped in the branches around them. The sun rose past the tree line and continued on its daily course. The stream parallel to the road gurgled faintly, just out of sight. But the longer they walked, the more the terrain changed. First small stones, then larger rocks littered the edges of the road. The level path gradually grew steeper and narrower. Just when Zed decided it was late enough that they should leave the road to avoid any potential travelers, it became entirely too late: the forest was so densely packed with enormous boulders that it was impassable. The road was their only option.

Soon the road, which had been climbing steadily uphill, leveled off. Instead, the terrain around them became steeper. As the path cut through the landscape they found themselves in a pass surrounded by sheer rockfaces twice as tall as they were.

"I don't like the looks of this," Zed muttered. "It's exactly the sort of place there'd be an ambush waiting in an old cowboy movie."

"Well, luckily we're not in an old cowboy movie," Tuesday replied. "We're just two regular kids, taking a stroll through an alternate dimension with our magic dog."

Zed would have appreciated her attempt to lighten the mood, except at that moment, he heard a sound that would have been very much at home in an old cowboy movie. Hoofbeats thundered on the path up ahead, raising a cloud of dust in the distance and grumbling like an approaching storm.

"Someone's coming!" he hissed at Tuesday. "What do we do?" The walls of the pass were too steep to climb. There was nowhere to hide.

"Just act casual!" Tuesday answered. "They'll probably just pass on by."

"Not when they see Nyx!" Zed looked around for the dog, but she was nowhere to be found. He caught movement out of the corner of his eye and looked up just in time to glimpse her tail disappearing out of sight on the ledge overhead.

Zed and Tuesday moved to one side of the path and held their breath as a party on horseback clattered into view. Zed's heart plummeted into his stomach as he recognized their orange tunics and black scaled armor. Soldiers. Of course.

The only soldiers they'd seen up until now had been in pairs, but the rapidly advancing group was impossible to count accurately in their dust cloud—maybe fifteen, Zed estimated. Before Tuesday could make out the figure engraved on their silver shoulder badges, their leader held up a fist to signal the others and reined his horse to a stop.

"What have we here?" said the man at the lead. The sun glinted off his bald head as he maneuvered his horse to block the road. His scraggly yellow beard was tied into a short, disheveled braid, which wobbled on his chin as he broke into a mocking grin. "Children, traveling alone? That doesn't seem...safe. Who knows what kind of villains you might run into?" A few of the soldiers behind him chuckled darkly.

"Children?" said a man at the back. "Let me have a look. Could be those fugitives Finnegan mentioned." His horse slowly pushed its way through the group until it stood at the first man's shoulder. This man was taller than the first, with long hair streaked with gray at the temples.

Tuesday stepped in front of Zed. She hunched her shoulders slightly and tilted her head to one side. "Gee, mister," she said, in a voice that sounded a bit higher to

Zed than normal, "We're just little kids. We don't know any fugitives. We were just heading to Kyoto to—"

"—to bring your sick Grandma some cookies, I suppose," he interrupted. "Don't take me for a fool, child."

"You stay and deal with them, then," the man with the braided beard ordered. "We need to make it to Etrusia before midday. Take a few soldiers for your detail and catch up with us when you can."

"Titus! Haldor! Malena! You're with me!" the second man barked. "Everyone else, with the company!"

A dozen soldiers thundered past on horseback. The cloud of dust they kicked up slowly settled around Zed, Tuesday, and the four soldiers who remained.

"Nice of the lieutenant to let me choose my own detail," the man commented once the rest of the group was out of sight. "Most members of the company don't share our…motivation."

He turned in his saddle to address one of the soldiers behind him. "So, what do you think, Titus?"

A lean, shifty-eyed man with a large crooked nose swung out of this saddle and approached Zed. "I'm not sure," he answered. "The boy doesn't look like I expected."

"You're blind if you can't see it," a dark-haired woman sneered. She directed her horse right in front of Tuesday and glared at her. "This one's the spitting image of Beren."

"Please! We don't know anyone named Beren!" Tuesday pleaded. "This is all a misunderstanding!"

"I don't think so," the woman said coldly. "But I know a way to find out."

She nodded at Titus. He pulled a polished silver cylinder out of a holster at his hip. As he held it up to Zed's neck, it became a sword.

"Lies and excuses don't last long, given the proper motivation." His voice was calm, smooth, almost bored. "So tell me—"

Zed didn't get to hear what he was supposed to tell him. The man's speech was interrupted by a deep, rumbling growl overhead. Everyone looked up; Nyx perched on the ledge above, drenched in blue flames, her glowing eyes fixed on the swordsman. She leaped down in front of Zed and Tuesday, forcing Titus to back away.

"Well, that settles it!" exclaimed the only soldier that had not yet spoken. "Leave it to Beren to come up with the unexpected. He went and found himself a Gabriel Hound!"

Titus turned back to mount his horse but found it had already fled. The other soldiers managed to control their mounts, but the horses stamped and reared; clearly they thought Titus's horse had the right idea. As Titus turned back to Nyx, brandishing his sword, the rest of the soldiers drew their weapons—the identical rods changed into a spiked ball on a chain, a spear, and a scythe.

"She's just defending us," Tuesday warned. "Let us pass, and she'll leave you alone. What do you want with us anyway?"

"You really think we care about you brats?" the woman laughed, tightening her grip on the scythe. "Don't flatter yourselves! It's your father we want."

Zed and Tuesday exchanged glances but said nothing.

"Your father is a traitor and a coward," she continued. "He betrayed his comrades, then fled to another world to escape our wrath. It took us sixteen years to track him down, but we'd pursue him if it took a hundred. We will not allow such injustice to go unpunished."

Their leader broke in. "We thought, surely, capturing his children would flush him out of hiding. But I don't see him anywhere, do you? Your father must be even more despicable than we thought! He'd rather save his own skin than defend you."

Tuesday's jaw clenched shut. A fire lit in her chest, raging, burning, threatening to consume her, a fire she was certain could only be quenched when those that insulted her father's character admitted their accusations lies and begged forgiveness on bended knees. She wanted to scream at them, but her fury defied words. As many times as she had suggested to Zed that their father might be a spy, or a kidnapper, or a criminal mastermind, she had thought only of the mystery and excitement of being swept into an adventure; now that she actually had been, all that melted away. Whatever he was involved in, whatever secrets he'd kept, Tuesday no longer cared—her concerns turned to dust in the heat of her righteous anger, leaving behind the glowing conviction searing her heart: her father was a good man.

Zed and Tuesday pressed their backs to the rock walls of the pass, waiting for Nyx to lunge at the soldiers, but to their surprise she did not. She crouched in front of them, growling and surveying her opponents for a moment, then abruptly extinguished the flames engulfing her. The glow in her eyes receded, fading back to their usual warm brown, and then continuing right on to black. A dark mist gathered around her. As it spread, Zed realized she was not exuding darkness at all—quite the opposite. Nyx was absorbing all the light around her, like a black hole. The soldiers took a step back, trying to escape the creeping void, but it was too late. Nyx, Zed, Tuesday, the soldiers, and their horses plunged into blackness.

Zed grabbed Tuesday's hand and laid his other palm flat against the rock wall. He had no idea whether Nyx could see in the dark cloud she had created or not, but from the alarmed shrieks of the horses and confused shouting of the soldiers, he knew at least he and Tuesday were not the only ones working blind. They walked as quickly and silently as they could, using the wall of the pass as a guide. Zed was not certain whether they were walking up the road towards Kyoto, or back the way they had come—not that it mattered, though. At the moment, anywhere was better than here.

It was an interesting sensation, this complete darkness. If he hadn't been fleeing for his life, Zed would have liked to just sit and absorb the experience. Any darkness he thought he had been in, until now—walking around the house at night, or hiding in a closet during a game of hide and seek—was as bright as a summer afternoon compared to this complete absence of light. He became newly aware of his heart drumming against his ribs, the slight breeze whisking past his skin, the rich, damp smell of the earth and trees. Although he had the rock wall to guide his way, he found it more difficult to keep his balance without any visual input. He almost felt as if the ground was swaying beneath his feet. Then, all of a sudden—he could not be imagining this part, could he? His knees collapsed under him as a slick fabric closed around his entire body. Tuesday's fingers slipped from his grasp. His weight was hoisted off the ground.

A hoarse whisper sounded in his ear. "Not one sound, if you want to live."

Chapter 14

ANOTHER UNFORTUNATE MEETING

Darkness. Well, that was nothing new. Of course it was dark. But now, it was dark not only because of Nyx, but also because Zed was tied up in a sack. A gripping, creaking sound—ropes? His weight was being pulled directly upward rather than bumping against the side of a person carrying him, so yes, probably ropes. The gripping sound continued for what seemed to Zed to be a very long time, though he supposed this was because he was straining to catch every clue as to what was going on; in reality, it was probably less than a minute. The sound stopped, and Zed swung gently in the air—they must have stopped pulling. The bag was jostled a bit, then bumped against something knobby—now he was being carried. Then the bag was hefted up, and he felt a hard, flat surface underneath him, too smooth to be the forest floor. His ears caught the snapping of twigs now and then—someone was walking nearby.

Zed could not tell how much time had passed, but gradually, the darkness inside the bag became less intense. It was still dark of course, but somehow less than the consuming blackness of before. There was a rustling sound above him as someone untied the sack.

Zed popped his head out of the bag and blinked into the welcome return of daylight. He was on a hover sled next to a second bag, which a teenage boy was busy untying. After fumbling with the rope for a moment, the boy was able to open it, and Tuesday's head emerged.

A man with a broad nose, deep amber skin, and dark, closely-cropped curls knelt next to the sled. "Sorry about that," he said with an apologetic smile that crept up to meet his eyes. "We couldn't risk being followed. You can step out of the bags now."

Half a dozen people stood around the sled. They were in the forest again, but it looked more like the terrain they had crossed yesterday, without so many of the boulders that had blocked their way this morning.

"Who are you?" Tuesday demanded. "Where are we? And why did you capture us?"

The man chuckled. "I'm afraid I'll be the one asking questions here. Now, who are you, and why were those soldiers so upset with you?"

Tuesday pressed her lips together, folded her arms defiantly, and looked away. Zed looked from Tuesday to the man and back again, not sure what to say, or whether to say anything at all.

"Well, if you won't tell me yourself, let's see what I can find out." The man nodded to a woman standing nearby. Two more men appeared behind the sled and pinned Zed and Tuesday's arms back while she turned out their pockets. The papers from Zed's cloak fluttered to the ground.

"There, that's more like it." The man unfolded the sheets and began reading. "Hmm..." He frowned. "Unusual pages you have here. Care to explain?"

Tuesday pressed her lips even more firmly closed.

"Where is Nyx?" Zed asked.

"Nyx? You mean the hound? Well, if she belongs to you, then I suppose we'll be seeing her shortly, won't we?"

"What's that supposed to mean?" Tuesday spat. "Are you planning to capture her too? Good luck with that."

The man laughed. "You've got fire—I admire that. But things really would go much more smoothly if we didn't repeat that incident with the soldiers. Once the hound is finished teaching them a lesson, I imagine her first order of business will be to track you two down, and it would be helpful if she didn't burst into flames when she gets here, so let's all just have a seat and try to look calm, shall we?" He sat down cross-legged on the ground and motioned to everyone else to do the same. The men holding Zed and Tuesday's arms back released them.

Zed turned to Tuesday and shrugged, then sat down. Tuesday glowered, but followed suit.

"So how did you find us, anyway?" Zed asked the man.

"Pure luck, actually," he admitted. "We were waiting on the ledge to interrupt the soldiers' convoy, but then you and that hound of yours proved much more interesting. As soon as she turned out the lights, we set up a few nets, and you walked right into them."

"But how could you have seen us? Everything was pitch black."

"Well, unlike the soldiers, we brought along a few of these." He reached over to the sled and pulled a pair of goggles out of another sack. "These visors allow us to follow the movement of air currents, even in the dark. Air doesn't move through solid objects, so the silhouette of any trees, rocks, or people we need to avoid—or find—stands out. Normally we use them for nighttime missions, but they came in quite handy today."

"Missions?" Zed pressed.

"Oh, I think I've talked enough about myself," he answered casually. "Either of you feeling more cooperative yet?"

"There's nothing to say!" Tuesday grumbled. "We were just walking along, minding our own business, and yours is the second group of people this morning hassling us for no reason."

"Come now," the man insisted, "do you really expect me to believe that? If the soldiers were that insistent about detaining you, then you aren't just regular children minding your own business. And it's not every day you see a Gabriel Hound, either."

"Well now you've seen one. Just let us go, and Nyx won't be your problem anymore!"

"I'm afraid I can't do that. My superiors will need to question you. Clearly, you have information you're hesitant to share, and if it's something that will help our cause, it's vital that we know it."

"And what 'cause' is that?" asked Zed.

"Perhaps when you feel like sharing a bit more, I will too," the man answered.

They sat in silence. While most of the people scattered among the trees scanned the area like nervous deer, their leader calmly observed Zed and Tuesday. After another ten minutes or so, Nyx came dashing up.

A few members of the party flinched, but the man just smiled as Nyx licked Zed's ear, then laid down next to him, panting.

"There now," he said. "All together again. Now we can continue on our way."

"On our way where?" Tuesday demanded.

"You'll see."

114

Chapter 15

THE HIDEOUT

"My name's Solomon, by the way," the man said as he motioned for everyone to rise. The woman who had searched them jumped onto the hover sled and drove in the lead, while everyone else followed on foot.

"And I suppose you expect me to introduce myself too, like a polite little girl?" Tuesday shot back.

"It would be nice to call you something other than 'hey you', but you'll be talking to my superiors whether you like it or not, so you may as well start now."

"Oh come on, what harm could it do?" Zed coaxed.

"Fine," she muttered. "I'm Tuesday, this is my brother Zed, and I guess we already let Nyx's name slip."

At the sound of her name, Nyx's ears perked up. She quickened her pace to catch up with Tuesday and nuzzled her wet nose into Tuesday's palm.

"She seems very devoted to you," Solomon observed. "To be honest, she's not quite what I expected. Gabriel Hounds have an intimidating reputation. Some reports are so far-fetched, in fact, that many people don't believe Gabriel Hounds exist at all, outside of campfire stories and children's bedtime tales."

Zed nodded. He wouldn't have believed the things Nyx had done the past few days either if he hadn't seen them with his own eyes.

The party trudged through the forest for another hour, passing countless trees, bushes, and rocks that all looked the same to Zed. They were not following any sort of trail that he could tell. The only thing that ever changed was a rushing sound that grew closer and closer with each step they took. Water, he thought, but not the cheerful gurgling of the stream he and Tuesday had followed before. This had more force behind it.

Much more, it turned out, as they stepped into a clearing. As the trees gave way to field, the hover sled led the way to a towering waterfall. Though they were on the other side of the field, they could already feel the spray misted into the air by the waterfall crashing against the rocks below. The river carved its way through the field, meandering back and forth until it continued out of sight. Zed wondered whether this river fed the smaller stream they had already encountered or took a different path entirely.

When they were so near to the waterfall that its spray was beginning to dampen their clothes, the woman driving the hover sled motioned for everyone to wait behind her. She carried on alone for a few yards, then pulled a long necklace chain out from under her cloak. A fat, silver ring was strung on the chain; as she grasped it in the fingertips of both hands, Zed realized it was not really one ring at all, but two, attached along a seam in the middle. She twisted the rings against each other, backward, forward, and backward again, like a combination lock. When she finished and tucked the chain beneath her cloak again, an astonishing thing happened: an enormous rock emerged from behind the water, right at the top of the falls, inching forward until it diverted the flow of the waterfall like a giant hand parting a curtain. Without a word, the woman motioned everyone forward.

"This is your hideout?" Zed asked. "If it's such a secret, why would you let us see it?"

Solomon chuckled. "Why, do you have any idea where we are?"

None at all, Zed had to admit. He had no idea how far, or in which direction, they had traveled while he was tied up in the sack. It was unlikely this was the only waterfall in Falinnheim. And even if he could find his way here again, who would he tell anyway?

"I had to bring your hound along—she would have followed us here in any case," Solomon explained. "And I couldn't blindfold you for the journey, or she would have retaliated. It's an acceptable risk."

The party formed a ragged line, scrambling single-file over the slick rocks revealed by the diverted waterfall, into a cavern hidden behind it. Zed wasn't sure what he had expected to see upon entering his captors' lair, but as his eyes adjusted to the dimmed light of the cave he was surprised by the sight that emerged: sodden papers littered the cave floor, chairs and desks were overturned, a large map on one wall was charred and torn. A few lights strung from the dripping rock ceiling flickered on and off at random intervals.

"Nice place you've got here," said Tuesday dryly. "Did you decorate it yourself?"

Solomon smirked a little but said nothing. He walked over to one side of the cave and pressed on a rock with his thumb, completely indistinguishable from any other rock jutting out of the cavern wall. A doorway appeared in the rockface and slid open. The woman driving the hover sled flipped a switch to turn it off; as it slowly eased itself down to the cavern floor, she and the rest of the group lined up behind Solomon, Zed, Tuesday, and Nyx.

The party filed into a tiny room. They all had to budge up against each other to fit, like in a packed elevator. Zed began to wonder if it actually might be some sort of elevator. The door sealed behind them as Solomon approached an illuminated control panel.

"Access code Solomon Eight Six Four," he recited into a speaker. He then held his left hand level with the panel, palm down; a red beam of light appeared and scanned the back of his hand from fingertips to wrist. The light disappeared, the control panel blinked a bit, and then a door next to the panel slid open.

"Dismissed," Solomon announced as the group filed past him through the door. Finally only Solomon, Tuesday, Zed, and Nyx remained. "After you," he said, ushering them on with a wave of his hand.

They stepped into a brightly-lit room bustling with activity. People hustled back and forth, papers in hand, taking no notice of the new arrivals. In one corner, a pair of robots shaped like domed barrels hummed in gradually shifting circles, polishing the slick white floors. A few people clustered around an array of screens completely covering one wall, apparently having some sort of meeting. Everything about the room was crisp, orderly, and busy. Aside from the lack of windows, there was no evidence that they were in a cave at all—more like a futuristic office building.

Solomon approached a desk manned by a hologram of a squat middle-aged woman, her round face crowned with a halo of chestnut-colored frizz. "We have guests," he announced to the flickering image, as casually as if he'd been addressing a living receptionist. "Please summon someone to show them to a waiting room and bring them something to eat. And let the chief know I'd like a quick word."

"Right away, Captain," the hologram responded. She closed her eyes for a few moments, then opened them again. "Attendants will be with our visitors momentarily. The General is expecting you."

Tuesday rolled her eyes at the irony of being referred to as a "visitor", given that she had absolutely no choice in the matter. Still, better than being tied up and shoved around, at any rate.

Momentarily, as the hologram had promised, two attendants arrived.

"Welcome!" beamed a young woman. "Please follow us this way and—" Her smile faded as her eyes drifted downward and landed on Nyx sprawled on the floor next to Zed's feet. The young man standing beside her said nothing, but took half a step back, his eyes widening.

"It will be fine," Solomon said, holding the woman's gaze. His voice was calm, but firm. "Please find their hound something to eat as well."

"Of…of course, Captain," she managed at last, with a weak smile.

"Right this way." Her partner made a sweeping gesture with his arm, directing Tuesday and Zed onward, but his eyes kept flicking involuntarily down at Nyx.

The pair led them down a hallway, around a corner, and finally to a small room with the door propped open.

It was completely bare except for a square wooden table and two chairs. Another young man appeared behind them carrying a platter of food and a metal pitcher. He slid the tray onto the table and left the room without comment.

"Please have a seat," the young woman bid them. "I'll return shortly with a meal for your…companion." And with that, the two attendants exited, closing the door behind them.

Nyx sniffed at all the corners of the room, then settled herself underneath the table. The first thing Tuesday had planned to do was try the doorknob, hoping against hope it wasn't locked, but as she turned around she realized their side of the door had no knob at all.

"So much for hospitality," she grumbled. "I don't care how they dress this situation up—we're not any sort of guests. We're prisoners."

"Nothing to do but wait." Zed sat in one of the chairs and selected a piece of bread and some grapes from the tray.

"What are you doing?" Tuesday hissed at him. "That could be poisoned!"

"If they meant to harm us, they've had plenty of chances before now," he reasoned. "We haven't had a decent meal in two days, and we have no idea when the next one might be. I'm not turning this one down." He popped a grape into his mouth with a grin.

"Fine," Tuesday grumped, pouring herself a glass of water and grabbing a wedge of cheese. "But if this is poisoned, I'm blaming you."

They chewed in silence. There was so much they might have discussed, but as Tuesday pointed out, their conversation was likely being monitored. Finally, the door opened and the attendant carried in a pair of metal bowls. She set them on the floor, then hurried back to the doorway.

Nyx's ears perked up. She shot out from beneath the table and launched herself at the bowls, wolfing down their contents with enthusiasm.

"Please come with me," the woman said, gesturing them out the door. "You will be reunited with your companion when she has finished her meal."

Solomon met them outside the door. "I'll escort them from here, Aletha."

A look of relief washed over the woman's face. She pulled the door shut behind them and scurried back up the hallway.

"Where are we going now?" Tuesday asked, scowling.

"You've been accorded a rare honor," Solomon said as he guided them down yet another corridor. "You're going to meet the Green Fly."

Chapter 16

THE GREEN FLY

"Where have I heard that name?" Zed mumbled to himself. He was certain he had heard of the Green Fly before, but where?

"Wanted poster," Tuesday whispered.

Right. On the bulletin board in New Angkor. At the time, he had imagined the Green Fly must be some sort of bandit, but if that was the case, this was the most well-organized band of robbers he'd ever heard of. What sort of thieves have captains and generals? Of course, the robots and holograms were out of the ordinary too, but after two days in Falinnheim relatively little surprised him anymore. A hidden lair behind a waterfall was more like it, though.

Solomon stopped at a door identical to all the others in the hallway and turned the knob. "I'll be waiting for you here," he said as he opened the door and showed them inside.

Tuesday and Zed stepped in. The door clicked shut behind them.

This room was only slightly larger than the last one they'd been locked in, and nearly as bare; a large clock on the wall behind them and a lamp in the corner were the only touches indicating this was a private office, and not a holding cell. There were no windows, no decorations, just a polished wooden desk facing the door. A woman sat behind the desk scribbling intently on a sheet of paper; a tall stack of documents waited at her elbow. All Zed and Tuesday could see of her, as she bent over her work, was the top of her head. Her silver hair, streaked here and there with a few darker strands, was knotted into a neat bun at the base of her neck, not a single hair out of place.

Tuesday and Zed stood silently, side by side, just inside the office door. The woman continued writing as though she had not noticed their entrance.

"Either the Legion is accepting younger recruits than I thought, or Solomon got a bit sidetracked today," she said at last, without looking up from her work. Her voice was as crisp and expressionless as the rest of her surroundings—not gruff, just unadorned and to the point. She finished the page and set it aside, then grabbed the next one from the top of the stack and carried on as before.

It was a statement, not a question; Tuesday got the

impression she had not expected a response. The ticking of the clock was the only sound punctuating the tense silence.

The woman finished this sheet, set it aside, then finally looked up. Her square jaw and tightly drawn lips gave the impression of a woman with no patience for distractions, and her curt demeanor made clear this was all she considered Zed and Tuesday to be. Delicate lines radiated from her eyes and the corners of her mouth, like hairline cracks in a porcelain mask. Not smile lines, though, Zed noted—not like Mrs. Alvarez had. These were cold.

"Explain your connection to the soldiers Captain Solomon's party encountered today," she said calmly. She laced her fingers together on the desktop and waited.

Zed turned to Tuesday, wondering what they should say, and found her face as still and expressionless as the woman's. So, they were going to have a showdown, then. Who would break first?

"How did you come to be traveling with a Gabriel Hound?" the woman tried next.

Tuesday stood firm.

The Green Fly waited.

Finally Zed couldn't take it anymore. "Answer our questions first," he blurted.

"Captured spies are in no position to make demands."

"We aren't spies!" said Tuesday.

At least we're getting somewhere, thought Zed.

The woman opened a desk drawer and pulled out

two creased, smudged sheets of paper, the same ones Solomon had confiscated from Zed earlier. "You were traveling alone, in the company of a malicious animal. You carried no supplies for a journey. You engaged in an altercation with law enforcement officials. And you were found to be carrying coded messages, which you refused to explain to my captain. How, precisely, does this differentiate you from spies?"

"We're just kids!" Tuesday protested. "How could we be spies?"

"Children make some of the best spies," she argued. "No one suspects them. We employ children to deliver messages and collect observations all the time."

The woman regarded Tuesday and Zed for a moment before continuing. "If you are simply delivering messages for someone else, perhaps you do not understand their contents. If that is the case, I could release you and pursue the agents responsible for the messages instead. Who gave you these pages, and where were you supposed to deliver them?"

"They weren't given to us, we just found them," Zed told her. "One page in New Angkor, and one in Persepolis." He decided to leave out the part about the sheep sign and the holograms, for now.

Tuesday shot him a betrayed look, which he ignored. "They weren't even hidden," he continued. "There were lots of copies."

"And why did you decide to collect them?" the woman prodded.

"We just thought they were interesting."

"Why?"

"Because we recognized the rhymes—nursery rhymes, they're called. Where we come from, small children are taught to recite them."

"For what purpose?"

Zed frowned. He didn't have an answer to that.

"Do nursery rhymes have a meaning?" the woman tried.

"Well…" Zed faltered. "Maybe they did, a long time ago? I'm not really sure. I don't think they mean anything to the children who learn them."

"Then why insist that children memorize them?"

Good question. "Tradition, I guess," he answered with a shrug.

The woman's voice became stern. "You're telling me you come from a place where even the youngest of children are instructed in codes, and you expect me to believe you are not spies? Where is it you come from, anyway?"

Zed declined to answer this, to Tuesday's relief.

"Is it also common for children to fraternize with demonic beasts where you come from?"

"Nyx is our pet," Zed replied simply.

The woman searched them with narrowed eyes, her lips stretched even tighter than before. The clock ticked steadily on, like a heartbeat.

"Captain!" she called at last.

The door opened, and Solomon appeared.

"Detain them," she ordered. "Perhaps they need a night to consider their options. They can answer my questions without omitting so many details, or they can sit in a holding cell until we discover the answers by our own means. But one way or another, I will learn the truth."

Solomon gave a crisp, silent nod and led them from the room.

"Who is that 'Green Fly' lady anyway?" Tuesday groused as Solomon led them back down the maze of hallways. "Some kind of spy? An interrogator? She's probably running off to see the General right now, to tell him every word we said."

"The General?" Solomon frowned for a moment, then gave a small chuckle. "Why, you just met her."

Chapter 17

TURNING THE TABLES

Tuesday and Zed were reunited with Nyx, just as Aletha had promised. She hadn't mentioned it would be in jail though—minor detail. But that was the Green Fly's decision, after all, Zed reminded himself. Aletha was just doing her job.

After they stopped by the first room to retrieve Nyx, Solomon directed them to another, very similar room. This one had no table or chairs, just three bedrolls on the polished white floor. There was another door at the back of the room though—that was different.

"I hope your accommodations will be adequate," Solomon said. "They're nicer than most of our agents have access to, in fact. The bathroom is through the door on the back wall. There's also a small laundry port inside— set your clothes in the port as you shower, and they'll be cleaned and ready before you are."

He turned to go but paused with his hand on the doorknob for one last word.

"I often find that getting myself cleaned up clears my head as well. I hope you'll reconsider your position—this situation could be mutually beneficial, if managed correctly." With a meaningful glance directed at Tuesday, he closed the door and was gone.

"Why'd you have to go and tell her so much?" Tuesday sulked once they were alone.

"Everything I told her was true, but she didn't really learn much from it," said Zed. "Besides, why are you so dead set on keeping secrets from her?"

"Because she's a bandit! Or a supervillain! Or… something." Tuesday realized they actually had no idea who they were dealing with. Still, her pride was at stake. She wasn't about to go spilling what few beans she had control of just because grownups she had never met ordered her to. In fact, Tuesday decided abruptly—yes. She would refuse to talk simply because they had ordered her to. "I don't care how that lady threatens us, I'm not saying another word."

"She hasn't actually threatened us," Zed pointed out. "I mean, we're locked up until we cooperate, but it's not like they're pulling out torture devices or anything."

"Yet," Tuesday added with a huff.

She stalked off to the bathroom. Part of her felt that accepting any hospitality from her captors was essentially giving in, which on principle she rarely did, and even then only on her own terms. But once Solomon mentioned the possibility of a shower, Tuesday became keenly aware of just how grimy the adventures of the last two days had left her. Every inch of exposed skin was coated in dust, she smelled like campfire smoke, her tennis shoes and the bottoms of her jeans were absolutely filthy where the cloak had not covered them, and most of all, Tuesday longed to brush her teeth. She ran her fingers self-consciously through her hair and discovered a dried leaf caught in a tangle at the back of her head.

Lights in the ceiling came on as she opened the door—not in a sudden click like in public restrooms back home, but silently and somewhat gradually, as though they took a moment to stretch and yawn before waking up. It was a small room, with walls, floor, and ceiling all covered in the same slick, white material as the base's hallways. One wall held a large mirror mounted above a sink. A toilet and shower stall and a couple of shiny metal hatches set into the wall next to the sink completed the room.

The sink, Tuesday noticed as she approached, had three different taps: the center one looked like a typical water faucet, with a handle to turn water flow on and off, but those on either side had a metal plunger like an old-fashioned typewriter key set into the top. The left spout, labeled SOAP, dispensed a squirt of something resembling whipped cream into the sink basin when she pressed the plunger. She rinsed it down the drain, feeling a bit sheepish that she hadn't thought to put her hand underneath to catch it before trying the button. The one on the right, labeled DENTAL, dispensed a single squishy bead that looked like a blueberry, except it was shiny and perfectly spherical. Tuesday hesitated a moment, but finally popped the bead into her mouth. It dissolved instantly, then expanded like shaving cream, foaming over her teeth and tongue, filling every crevice of her mouth. She spit it out into the sink in alarm—and was astonished to note that her teeth were no longer upholstered in gunk. She had to admit that Falinnheim's alternative to the toothbrush was efficient, even if the sensation had caught her by surprise.

She undressed, taking note of a few new bruises on her arms and legs, and deposited her clothes into one of the metal hatches, a recessed area in the wall about the size of a microwave. The door was embossed with the word LAUNDRY. The moment she closed the hatch a slight puffing noise ensued, and the seams of the door emitted faint wisps of purple steam. The other hatch, directly below, was identical in size and shape, except it was labeled GARBAGE.

After Tuesday finished her shower (this, at least, had looked familiar to her, although no soap or shampoo were provided—the water that trickled out of the faucet in the ceiling seemed to have some kind of cleaning solution already added) she found her clothes in the laundry hatch waiting for her, clean and warm, just as Solomon had promised. No towels were provided either, but the hairbrush she discovered hanging from a hook in the shower area had dried her hair instantly as she tugged it through her tangles, so Tuesday decided the towel oversight could be forgiven. She dressed, then returned to the adjoining room, flopping down on her bedroll to scratch Nyx's ears while she waited for Zed to take his turn in the bathroom.

He returned after what seemed to Tuesday to be an unnecessarily lengthy wait. She had no way of measuring exactly how long Zed had been in there of course, but however long it had been, she was certain he should have returned long before she felt impatient. It would only have been common courtesy.

"Hey, did you try out those mouthwash berry thingies?" Zed commented when he finally emerged. "They taste like…well, I couldn't place the flavor, actually. Lemon? But not that 'zingy'. Like a lemon cream frosting, I guess, but now that I think of it, it definitely wasn't sweet either…"

Tuesday was stunned. She hadn't even noticed how the exploding foam bead had tasted. But of course, she wasn't about to admit to that.

"Lemon?" she scoffed. "Why would something blue taste like lemon? I think you need to get your taste buds checked."

"Blue? Cool, mine wasn't blue! Although it wasn't really yellow either. More of a pale cream color? I hadn't even considered they might not all be the same. I'm gonna go try another!"

"Will you quit having so much fun?" Tuesday snapped. "We are prisoners, not tourists!"

"Well grumping about it won't change anything. Honestly Tuesday, this place is amazing! How can you sit there sulking at a time like this? We're in a futuristic medieval secret hideout military spy base! What, would you rather be in school right now, in our boring, normal town?"

"Or in our boring, normal house?" Tuesday whispered gravely. "With our boring, normal parents?"

Oh. Zed had been so busy reveling in all the novelties Falinnheim had to offer that he hadn't considered Tuesday might view their situation through a different lens. He sat down next to Tuesday and put his arm around her shoulders. Neither said anything for a long time.

"Look, let's just go over what we know," Zed suggested at last.

"If you want," Tuesday sighed glumly.

"Well, we know that this organization, whatever it is, is not on the same side as the soldiers. People in the villages seem afraid of the soldiers. But only a few of them, like the ones who stopped us this morning, are mad at—"

"Sshhhh!" Tuesday frantically put a finger to her lips. "We don't know who's listening!"

"Fine," Zed sighed. "Only some of the soldiers are mad at that person we know, for reasons they didn't fully explain."

"Yeah, what do you think about that?" Tuesday frowned. "Do you think they've got the wrong person? What if they're right? I just can't believe what they said about…you know, him."

"Well, we can ask him all about it when we get home. Let's not forget our goal here. The messages, traveling to the different villages—the entire purpose is to find our way back. All the rest of this stuff we've gotten tangled up in is beside the point."

"Yeah, but is it?" asked Tuesday. "We don't know who sent the messages. We're not actually certain they were meant for us. The only person who seemed to have any answers about why we're here is the man with the broken compass, and he wasn't very talkative either. Even if these people released us right this minute, all we could do is stumble blindly around after Nyx again. We really don't know much about what's going on."

Zed sat hunched on his bedroll, arms around his knees, and thought for a while before he spoke again. "You know, I think we've been going about this the wrong way."

"What do you mean?"

"We've been treating Solomon and the Green Fly like they have the upper hand."

Tuesday motioned around them. "In case you haven't noticed, we are in jail. Sure looks like they have the advantage here."

"We're in jail because they really, really want some answers. Answers we have."

"I really don't see how what little we know is helpful to them…"

"Doesn't matter. They want to understand the messages, and we do. We want to know more about who they are, and how the soldiers fit into the picture. If we play our cards right, we may just have the leverage we need to get that information."

"You mean…we need to bluff." A grin crept over Tuesday's face. "I like it."

"I'd like to think of it as calling their bluff, but sure. It's time to turn the tables."

"I can do that," Tuesday said, nodding. "This might even be fun."

Chapter 18

A HISTORY LESSON

"Hey! Guard!" Tuesday shouted at the ceiling. "We want to talk to the General again!"

Silence. One minute, two, then—the door swung open. So, someone was listening. Interesting…

They had expected to find Aletha behind the door, eager to show them around like a cheerful game show host, or at least her solemn butler of a partner. Instead, they were met by a guard they'd never seen before. His tall, squarely-built frame filled the entire doorway, so that he had to duck a little to avoid hitting his head, and his expression was as somber as a raincloud. He closed the door behind them and gestured them silently forward. Right, left, down a long corridor, left again, then finally to the General's door. He opened the door, showed them inside, and closed them in.

The General was still behind her desk, still surrounded by stacks of papers, but this time she cut right to the chase.

"I understand you have something to share with me," she said, "and that for some unimaginable reason, you feel qualified to make demands."

Tuesday took a step forward. "You were right," Tuesday announced. "Absolutely right. The pages Solomon took from us really are secret messages. And we understand the code. We know exactly what the messages say. In fact, we understand the messages so well that we didn't even bother writing down the fourth one."

The General's eyebrows shot up. "Fourth?"

"That's right," Tuesday continued. "We collected two pages, wrote one message down on the back of a sheet, and there's one more you don't even know about. We have it memorized."

"You're bluffing."

"I'm not. We have four secret messages that only we can decode."

"My cryptographers may not have cracked the code yet, but it's a little bold to insist no one ever could. Now I know you're bluffing."

"The code is completely unbreakable, because it depends on knowing the rhymes in advance. If you don't know the rhyme, you'll never understand what the code says."

Tuesday and the General regarded each other for a moment.

"The rhyme itself has no meaning?" the General asked. "'Jack and Jill' and 'the king' are not code names for agents, or targets, for example?"

"Nope. Not even close."

Another moment of silent staring.

"I assume you're not telling me this because you've suddenly decided to be cooperative," the General sighed.

"Right again," said Tuesday.

Zed was glad he had left this part of the plan to Tuesday; she was really getting into this. In fact, there was an eerie similarity to the way Tuesday and the General bantered back and forth, leveraging their information, each trying to dig something new out of their opponent without exposing any weakness in themselves. It was like watching a game of tennis, or a fencing match.

"What do you want?" the General said at last.

"We want to know who you are, and what sort of outfit you're running here," Tuesday deadpanned. "Why you're ambushing soldiers, and kidnapping children, and building secret hideouts. If your answers are satisfactory, we will explain the messages to you, and then you will send us on our way."

"If I agree to explain all of that," the General answered, "and that's a very big if—I'll want the same information from you. Who you are, where you're heading, why you understand secret messages, and how you came to be in control of a Gabriel Hound."

Tuesday considered for a moment before turning to Zed. He nodded.

"Agreed."

The General instructed the guard outside the door to bring three more chairs to her office. "And ask Captain Solomon to join us," she added. "He may as well hear the rest of the story firsthand, instead of in a briefing meeting later."

When Solomon appeared moments later, followed by two assistants, each was carrying a cushy purple armchair. "They were going to bring the wooden chairs from a waiting room," he explained, "but I insisted on these. It sounds like we have a lot to discuss." They set the seats down in a cluster in front of the General's desk, then the assistants slipped out as Solomon selected one of the chairs and settled in. The General suppressed a weary smile and, after brief consideration, slid her chair out from behind her desk to join them. It was more like a conversation now, with everyone sitting in a circle, and less like an interrogation. Zed suspected this was exactly what Solomon had intended.

"So, let's hear it," the General said to Zed and Tuesday. "How does the code work?"

"Not so fast!" Tuesday parried. "You first."

"What do you expect, my life story?"

"We just want to know who we're dealing with," Zed explained. "We don't want to turn over all this information without some idea what you're going to do with it." He didn't really think what little information they had was much use to anyone but themselves, but no need to show that hand just yet.

The General turned to Solomon. "I'll let you do the honors, Captain."

Solomon leaned forward in his chair, resting his forearms on his knees. "In short, we are trying to overthrow the government."

"What!" Tuesday yelped. "And you expect us to help you?"

"Let me explain," he soothed. "You're too young to remember this, but Tyrren hasn't always been in charge around here. For most of Falinnheim's history, we've been led by a council comprised of an extended royal family—the Regents Council, it was called. The oldest member of the clan served as the Moderator, leading discussions and giving counsel, but had no real power to make decisions. The princes and princesses of the Council made governing decisions together, usually calling experts from the community to advise them on particular issues. This kept any one person from having too much power, and from passing laws that were unwise or selfishly motivated. But then Tyrren staged a coup, killing the entire royal family and placing himself in charge. He calls himself the Liberator, for 'freeing' Falinnheim from monarchy, but in reality he just became a dictator."

"So…where do you fit in?" Tuesday wanted to know.

"We are the resistance movement trying to stop him," said Solomon. "Not only did he murder the entire Regents Council, but he brutally silences anyone who opposes him in any way. Anyone who complains about a law, or about his takeover in general, or even asks too many questions—they disappear, never to be seen again. We've spent more than a decade doing what we can to get him out of power. We started small—just a handful of people who could see through his plans and had the courage to do something about them. But as you can see, we're not so small anymore."

"So, those soldiers we met today—they're kidnapping people for Tyrren?" Zed asked.

The General let out a bitter laugh. "Those clods? No. The Legion is just local law enforcement. I doubt most of them have even met Tyrren. Some have gotten a bit corrupt, harassing villagers and running protection rackets and the like, but they're not actually in that much power. No, it's the Red Hand that does Tyrren's bidding—his secret police. Officially, they don't exist at all, of course, but we've uncovered quite a bit of information about them. They serve as Tyrren's personal guards, and do whatever he tells them, unaccountable to anyone else."

"Then…if the soldiers aren't really involved in

Tyrren's plans, why follow them around?" Zed asked. "Shouldn't you be focusing on the Red Hand instead?"

"The soldiers might not know anything of Tyrren's plans," the General explained, "but he still controls them. They're the pawns in his game, you see, maintaining some semblance of order so Tyrren can work behind the scenes. He couldn't keep up his charade of bringing peace and liberty to the people if everything was in chaos. And whether they realize it or not, the soldiers are the ones who keep the Red Hand informed about local troublemakers who might pose a threat." The General paused for a moment, frowning. "I'd be delighted to focus on the Red Hand, if we knew who any of them are," she admitted reluctantly.

"So you can see," Solomon broke in, "how important it is that we make use of all the information we can find in pursuit of our goal—restoring Falinnheim to real freedom, not just Tyrren's false claims of liberty."

"But if the royal family is all dead, what would you do if you could manage to overthrow him?" Tuesday pointed out. "If you put yourselves in power in Tyrren's place, that's no better than what he did!"

"We'll cross that bridge when we come to it," said the General. "Calling a representative from each village to form a new Regents Council was one idea. The point is, we can't sit back and do nothing, or people will just keep on dying.

"And now," she continued, "it's your turn. How did you come across those messages, and how is it that you know how to decode them?"

"What we told you before was the truth," said Zed. "We found the messages and recognized them as nursery rhymes young children learn. Except, they had been modified a little. A few words in each rhyme have been changed. If you know how the rhyme is supposed to go, then you'll know which words were changed. The new words, strung together, form a message."

The General returned to her desk and pulled the rhyme pages out of a drawer. She passed them to Zed and handed Tuesday a pen. "Translate," she ordered. "And write down this fourth message you mentioned, and its translation."

Zed and Tuesday pulled their heads together, Zed watching as Tuesday circled words. She handed the pen to Zed, and he copied down the message from the sign at the crossroads, circling the changed words.

Zed passed the pages back to the General. He was amused to see the General and Solomon pull their heads close, just as he and Tuesday had, to review them. Finally the General thrust the papers into Solomon's hand in disgust.

"Is this some kind of joke?" Her voice rattled with the effort of containing her anger. "Keep hidden? Work together? Follow the dog? These aren't helpful at all!"

"You're the one who insisted they were important!" Tuesday retorted. "We never claimed it was super-secret spy stuff! You wanted to know what the messages said, and there it is—you can't blame us if you're disappointed!"

Solomon flipped the sheets over, reading and rereading the circled words. "The dog knows what?" he murmured. "Is this a reference to your hound?"

"Well…that's what we wondered," said Zed. "Tuesday and I seemed to be the only ones who understood the messages, and we did have our dog with us, so…"

"So you assumed the messages were meant for you," Solomon finished for him. "Any idea who created these messages? Who has a need to communicate with you? And why such secrecy?"

"I wish we knew," Zed sighed.

"You're leaving out a big part of this puzzle." The General scowled. "Why are you the only ones who understand the messages? You insist all children know these rhymes, but none of my cryptographers has ever heard of them."

"Well…" Zed glanced at Tuesday for guidance. "That's where things get complicated."

"Enlighten me," said the General dryly.

"We're not from Falinnheim," Tuesday replied with a shrug.

Chapter 19

CONNECT THE DOTS

Solomon met this news with a rapid succession of faces. First, one eyebrow arched in disbelief. Then he squinted slightly, looking down as if his knees might offer some sort of explanation. Momentarily, his face relaxed into an expression of patient interest. He clasped his hands together in front of him like a toddler waiting to be read a bedtime story, turning from Zed to Tuesday and back again.

The General, on the other hand, simply exploded. "What do you mean, you're not from Falinnheim?" she sputtered. "Now you're just spouting nonsense. Everything is Falinnheim. Even if you traveled here from one of the Outland islands, it's all still Falinnheim! Are you planning to tell me you're from the moon or something?"

Tuesday glanced at Zed with a mischievous grin, which Zed understood at once—she was considering stringing the General along for a while by telling her just that. He decided to intervene before Tuesday enraged the General even more.

"We don't really understand it ourselves," he explained. "We had never even heard of Falinnheim until a couple days ago. Two men attacked us in our home, we escaped, there was a beam of light, and suddenly we found ourselves in the woods outside New Angkor. A man there said he had brought us to Falinnheim to protect us from our attackers, handed us cloaks, and basically told us to get lost."

"And how did you meet the Gabriel Hound?" asked the General.

"Oh, she came with us, from home." Zed answered. "Like we said, she's been our pet for as long as we can remember. We had never heard of Gabriel Hounds until everyone here seemed afraid of her. We just thought she was an ordinary dog."

Tuesday rolled her eyes at this. Even at home, Nyx was not what anyone would call an "ordinary" dog, due to her size if nothing else. She was a bit embarrassed they had never been more suspicious about Nyx's peculiar abilities before—operating controls in a parked car, opening the refrigerator…but of course, what possible explanation would they have had?

The General also looked incredulous. Her expression made it clear she thought anyone who could mistake a Gabriel Hound for a house pet must suffer from a special brand of ignorance.

"Who was this man you mentioned?" Solomon asked. "The one who brought you here. And what do you mean by that, anyway? How was he able to move you from your home to New Angkor?"

"He had some sort of…device, I guess?" Zed ventured. "We'd never seen anything like it. Sort of a round, shiny thing like a compass, but more complicated. It broke shortly after we arrived, and he said it couldn't be used anymore."

"Does this man have a name?" The General asked.

"He called himself Scrimbley," said Tuesday. "Probably lying. Everything else about him was sketchy—I wouldn't be surprised if he gave us a fake name."

"Scrimbley?" Solomon looked dumbfounded. "Scrimbley the Enterprising? But…he's just a common swindler. Sells second-hand items that 'fell off the back of a sled', convinces gullible visitors they need to buy a permit from him to set up a stall at the village market, that kind of thing. Where did he get a device powerful enough to…bring you from…wherever it is you come from…" he trailed off.

"See?" Tuesday turned triumphantly to Zed, smacking him on the arm. "Told you we couldn't trust him!"

"Fascinating…" Solomon murmured to himself.

"I'm familiar with him," the General said

dismissively. "I suppose I could send a party out to interview him, but he'll be difficult to find, and whatever information he gives us is unlikely to be the truth. I certainly wouldn't want to bring him back here for interrogation—he'd share anything he learned about us with the first person to wave an eight-hour coin under his nose."

Tuesday sat back in her chair with a smug grin.

"Now, about the Legion," the General continued.

Tuesday's grin evaporated.

"I think it's safe to assume that the men who first attacked you are soldiers. Scrimbley claims he helped you escape them, but given he had the only transporting device we're aware of, it is likely he helped the soldiers reach you in the first place."

"Yeah, he pretty much admitted that already," said Zed. "Said they forced him to do it."

"Then why did he rescue you? Why turn against the Legion, if he was so afraid of them? More importantly, what did the Legion want with you in the first place?"

Tuesday's eyes stung. She stared at the ceiling, blinking back tears, defying them to reveal her darkest fears to people she barely knew.

"They…they said it had something to do with our father." Tuesday's voice came out strangled, like the words were escaping her mouth against her will. "The soldiers we met today, as well as the two in our house. They said…they…"

Zed put a hand on Tuesday's knee. "They said they knew our father a long time ago, and that they were angry with him."

"He was a criminal they were trying to arrest?" the General asked.

Tuesday shook her head in silence, still gazing at the ceiling.

"He fought against them somehow? Like our agents do?"

Zed sighed. "They called him a…traitor. They claimed that he betrayed them, and then ran away. That they were only interested in us because they were trying to get to him. For revenge, or something."

"Not revenge." Tuesday locked eyes with the General, her voice steely. "It was a trap—and we were supposed to be the bait."

The General was silent for a moment. Zed thought he saw the briefest flicker of concern cross her face—something in the momentary reflex of her eyebrows. Concern, or—could it be, sympathy?

"So your father is a former member of the Legion, then," she concluded quietly.

Zed and Tuesday said nothing. Tuesday's jaw clenched. Solomon leaned forward with his chin resting on his steepled fingertips, lost in thought.

"Where is your father now?" the General asked.

Zed and Tuesday said nothing.

Chapter 20

EXPERIMENTAL FAILURE

Tuesday was the one to break the painful silence. "Are we free to go, then?"

The General's pause before responding was a bit too long for Zed's liking. "Of course. We had a bargain, after all. Captain Solomon will make arrangements to transport you to—well, where would you prefer? The road you came from, or on to Kyoto?"

Zed's face fell as he realized why the General's response made him wary. He shook his head. "Tuesday, we can't leave," he sighed.

"What? Why not?" Tuesday asked, alarmed.

Zed sighed again. How could he not have seen it before? If their entire encounter with Solomon and the General had been a chess game, then he and Tuesday had been in check for the last three moves. His gambit to get them out of their cell had been entirely useless.

"If we leave," Zed explained heavily, "they'll just have us followed. We didn't really know why we were heading to Kyoto anyway, but whoever or whatever we found there, they'd just have intercepted. They may not care about Dad's feud with the Legion, but the prospect of inter-dimensional travel is just too useful to them to pass up."

Tuesday turned an accusing glare on the General. The General looked placidly back. And that was all the confession Tuesday needed.

"You're very perceptive," the General remarked to Zed. "I must say I'm impressed. If you do not wish to leave, you are welcome to remain here. I don't intend to abandon unsupervised children in an unfamiliar town against their will."

"So, we're your prisoners?" Tuesday gasped. "That wasn't our deal at all!"

Solomon hastened to reassure her. "You'll have to remain in a private room, for Nyx's sake if nothing else, but you're not captives. Think of it more like...protective guardianship. You're hardly alone in this situation—believe it or not, there are lots of people living here simply because they have nowhere else to go. You'll be housed and fed and can spend your time helping out in our support division. And if you decide later you'd rather continue on to Kyoto, we'll arrange it."

Tuesday stood. She opened her mouth, closed it, opened it again, and finally flounced off to the door. Solomon and Zed followed her out of the General's office.

"How did you know the General's plan?" Tuesday whispered to Zed as Solomon led them back to the room where they'd left Nyx. "It was like you could read her mind or something!"

Zed shrugged. "It's exactly what I'd do if I were in her place."

They returned to find Nyx sleeping on her back on Tuesday's bedroll, legs sprawled in the air like a dead cockroach, one of her paws twitching slightly. As they entered the room she opened her eyes, still upside down, then yawned and scrabbled to her feet to greet them. She stood and shook herself from shoulders to tail, dusting Tuesday's pillow with a confetti of wiry black hairs.

"Get some rest, for now," Solomon said. "Dinner will be brought to you shortly. Tomorrow morning I'll send someone along to show you around the support division." He turned to leave but paused with his hand on the doorknob. "Please try to see this from our perspective," he reasoned, his eyes imploring Tuesday to understand. "The work we do here is important. We really are the good guys, you know."

The door clicked shut, and they were alone again.

"That's exactly what the bad guys would say," Tuesday said with a scowl.

While that night was by far the most comfortable Zed and Tuesday had yet passed in Falinnheim, it was not without certain drawbacks. True, there was no longer any need to hide from the locals, scrounge for food, or sleep in the dirt. Their stomachs were full, their clothes were clean—they even had actual pillows! But as Tuesday reminded Zed at every opportunity, these comforts did not make up for the fact that they were no longer at liberty to—well, to do anything, really. Their door remained locked, except for the brief intervals when someone came by to deliver a meal. While the lights in the bathroom turned on and off automatically when needed, the lights to their sleeping quarters were apparently on a timer, or else controlled by a guard somewhere else in the facility. Sometime after they finished eating dinner, they began to notice that the lights were gradually dimming. Over the course of what Zed estimated to be half an hour they faded entirely, until they were left with no choice but to turn in for the night. In the morning, the same process had played out in reverse; the room gradually became brighter and brighter, goading them out from under their blankets to begin the day. Tuesday took these infringements on her independence as personal insults—they weren't even being trusted with a light switch! But Zed was really more concerned by the roadblock the situation had raised to their progress. You can't "follow the dog" anywhere if you aren't allowed to leave your room.

Just as they were wiping the breakfast crumbs from their faces, there was a knock at the door. They couldn't answer the door, of course, as their side of the room had no doorknob. But still—a knock! The guards delivering meals hadn't bothered, they just barged in and left a tray on the floor as near to the door as possible before exiting without a word.

"Uh…come in?" Tuesday called.

The door opened. A young man appeared—Zed guessed he was about twenty—followed by a woman roughly the same age. They were identically dressed in starched knee-length blue robes, belted at the waist, over loose brown leggings and tall leather boots. But aside from their clothing, they could not have looked more different. The man was only a few inches taller than Tuesday and kept unconsciously tucking unruly tufts of blonde hair back in place behind his ears. The woman was taller, with a few stray black curls peeking out at the forehead from under an emerald-green scarf, which was wrapped tightly over the top of her head and tied into an elaborate knot behind her neck. She extended her hand to Tuesday.

"So nice to meet you! My name is Fatima, and this is Orion." She beamed, gesturing briefly towards the man with her free hand. "We were asked—"

"—assigned," Orion cut in.

She rolled her eyes at him and continued. "—to escort you around today."

Tuesday offered a limp handshake to demonstrate her level of enthusiasm. Zed stepped forward to shake Orion's hand; the man grasped Zed by the forearm, rather than the palm, and withdrew after a brief squeeze.

"No one else was willing to take the assignment when they heard 'Gabriel Hound,'" Orion said with a lofty air. "Not sure what all the fuss was about, myself."

"Well, I volunteered," Fatima retorted. "I was a child as well when I first came to this base. I'm sure your first impression of life here must have been a bit intimidating; I hope after you have a chance to tour the inner workings of the place today, you'll feel a bit more comfortable."

Nyx trotted up and sat at Fatima's feet. Fatima patted Nyx's head gingerly and, seeing no dramatic reaction, gave her a scritch under the chin for good measure. Nyx then wandered over to sniff at Orion's boots.

"See—nothing to be afraid of," Orion remarked, as though addressing whoever had declined the assignment earlier. He did not go so far as to pet Nyx, however.

Fatima fished a clear glass sphere about the size of a plum out of a pocket of her robe and held it in her palm, consulting it like a wristwatch. "The schedule indicates you have a meeting in the research department in just a few minutes, so we should get started. Please roll up your sleeping mats and place them near the door. The cleaning pods will be making their rounds while we're gone; best to give them a clear path."

Zed and Tuesday did so, then followed Orion and Fatima into the hall.

"Should we leave Nyx here, or…?" Zed asked, looking up at Fatima.

"Oh! The hound—no, she needs to come along. The meeting is for her, in fact; we couldn't very well leave her behind. Actually, I've been instructed that she should stay with you at all times from here on out. I think they're a bit worried about what she might do in your absence, to be honest."

The research department consisted of a single large room, mostly empty but for a bank of instrument panels covered in knobs, buttons, and display screens. Four or five people in white robes crowded around the panel, adjusting settings. They pulled transparent visors over their faces as Orion led the party in but kept right on working.

"Right, then," one man called over. "We'd like to ask you a few questions about your Gabriel Hound and see some of its abilities in action, if possible. Please stand right there—not too close, now."

Zed and Tuesday stood. Orion and Fatima edged over to a corner of the room, out of the way of whatever experiment the researchers might have planned. Nyx trotted in random loops, nose to the ground, taking in all the new smells.

They tried their best to answer all questions the researcher lobbed at them: about Nyx's age, her eating habits, her temperament. No, to their knowledge, she had never had any sort of illness or injury. They had never seen her interact with any other Gabriel Hounds. She had never been known to fly, levitate, or become invisible (although Zed wasn't quite sure how anyone could guarantee an answer to that last condition.) Yes, she was capable of crossing streams, and could come into contact with water without harm.

Many of the questions they simply had no way of answering—they had no idea, for example, whether Nyx would be drawn to or repelled by the boundaries of a graveyard. They recounted any unusual ability she had demonstrated—controlling electrical devices, shocking fish in a stream, creating a field of darkness, and of course the blue flames. That generated follow-up questions the researchers had apparently not thought to ask the first time—no, to their knowledge, Nyx could not shoot flame balls, create lightning, or control tornadoes, earthquakes, or volcanoes.

"Right, then," the researcher said again when he'd run out of things to ask. "Please instruct the hound to demonstrate its fire abilities."

The other researchers looked up from the instrument panel and took a few steps back. One woman who had neglected to flip her protective visor down over her face earlier did so.

"Well you see, the thing is…" said Tuesday, "Nyx doesn't exactly follow instructions, for the most part."

"Well then how did you command it to perform the actions you described?"

"She…well, she mostly just does things on her own, when she decides she has a reason to."

"You mean you're traveling with a beast you're not even in control of?"

For a man who seemed open to the possibility that Nyx could create volcanoes or disappear entirely, he was awfully closed-minded on the issue of Nyx being used as a tool, rather than having her own will, Zed decided privately.

"Could it be controlling you?" the researcher wondered aloud.

"What? No!" Tuesday's patience was wearing thin. "And she has a name, you know—quit calling Nyx 'it!'"

"Can you make it do anything?" he pushed, ignoring Tuesday's comment.

"It's worth a shot, at least," Zed encouraged her.

"Ugh, fine," Tuesday muttered. "Nyx! Come!" she called.

Nyx continued sniffing in a far corner of the room.

"Sit!" Zed tried next.

Nyx looked up, then went right back to investigating smells.

"Play dead!"

Nyx sat down and began scratching vigorously at one ear with her back paw.

The researcher finally had enough. "All our previous study on Gabriel Hounds indicates that they form a bond with their master—one that practically forces them to obey their master's commands. If you cannot compel it to obey, then it's clear that this is not really your Gabriel Hound at all."

"Well, I could've told you that!" Tuesday huffed, but the man was no longer listening. He motioned to Orion and Fatima to remove Zed and Tuesday from the lab. As Orion held the door open, Nyx abruptly looked up and bounded over, her toenails clattering on the slick floors.

"Well, I suppose that makes sense," Fatima commented as she led them down the hall. "From the briefing I received this morning, it sounds like your father is the one who'd want a powerful creature at his command. It wasn't very fair to assume the hound was yours."

Zed and Tuesday made silent eye contact behind Fatima's back. They knew Fatima and the researcher were both wrong. But they had not realized until just now what the truth might mean.

A Summary of Nyx's Qualities
Recorded after the fact, for posterity
By Zed

Basic Stats
- Age: ??? At least 12 years
- Diet: whatever she can steal (sandwiches, mostly. Also: unspecified Falinnheim fish and birds. Definitely not dog kibble.)
- Temperament: friendly if calm, fiery and violent if threatened. Sleeps a lot (on back, mostly.)

Things the Resistance Scientist Thinks Gabriel Hounds Can Do
- ~~Fly~~ (nope)
- ~~Levitate~~ (nearly the same thing as above)
- ~~Turn invisible~~ (but how would we know?)
- Cross running water (she's not a vampire!)
- Get wet (keeping her dry is the problem! Note: smells funny when wet)
- Enter cemeteries (why??? Need more data)
- Stay out of cemeteries (see above)
- ~~Shoot flameballs~~ (awesome!!! But no. Note: would have come in handy earlier)
- ~~Create lightning~~ (someone's been reading too many comic books)

- ~~Control tornadoes, earthquakes, and/or volcanoes~~ (see above)
- ~~Follow commands~~
- Unusual bond with one person

Things Typical Dogs Can Do
- ~~Sit~~ (at least not on command)
- ~~Stay~~ (see above)
- ~~Shake~~
- ~~Roll over~~ (unless in something smelly)
- ~~Fetch~~ (sandwiches and dead birds, but not on command)
- ~~Follow directions of any kind~~
- Chase cats and squirrels
- Go on car rides
- Steal sandwiches
- Bite bad guys (Note: not gender specific)

Things Nyx Can Do
- Go flamey when threatened (Note: blue)
- Snort sparks to start campfires
- Send out electric shocks? (Only observed in water, need more data)
- Absorb light in her proximity

Chapter 21

BEHIND THE SCENES

The support division, Fatima explained, was not really one area of the base at all, but encompassed all the duty stations whose main function was to keep the others running smoothly. Their tour began in the kitchens, where people worked nearly around the clock to prepare meals for all the people working at the base. The workers in white aprons took no notice of them, but continued bustling about stirring huge vats of soup and pulling steaming trays of fresh rolls out of gigantic ovens set into the wall. Nyx scanned the floor for crumbs but trotted reluctantly after the others when she found none. After a quick stroll through the empty dining hall Orion led them to the repair bay, where everything from malfunctioning display screens and hologram projectors to wobbly table legs and holey socks were sent to be maintained, oiled, stitched, tightened, recalibrated, or programmed.

It was a large, well-lit room, with workbenches and stools lining the walls. At one workstation an old man, two middle-aged women, and to Zed's surprise, a boy who could not have been older than seven were working together to unscrew a cracked wheel from the bottom of one of the floor-polishing robots they had noticed when arriving with Solomon the day before. One woman held the robot on its side on the workbench, while the other kneeled on the floor to get a better view of the wheel.

"That's it, counter-clockwise, nearly there," she coached the boy, who was struggling to keep a good grip on the tool he was using to remove the wheel.

The old man walked to a display panel on a nearby wall and pushed a few buttons until the screen showed a picture of the exact size and shape of replacement wheel he needed. A hatch below the screen opened, dispensing the wheel, which he brought back to the workbench and handed to the boy.

"I'm confused," Tuesday said to Orion. "I thought this was some kind of military base or spy hideout or something. The research department and guards and stuff were all about what I expected, but why are there cooks and repair workers and kids here too?"

"Oh, you haven't seen anything yet," Orion answered as he led them back out of the repair bay. "We still haven't gotten to the garden wing, the crystal mine, the poultry yard—”

"The Resistance is primarily focused on their mission to restore Falinnheim to justice and peace," Fatima clarified, cutting him off, "but it takes a lot of work behind the scenes to support all the planning and missions and raids. Besides that, most people who join the Resistance do so because they simply can't go home anymore—because they'd be arrested for speaking out against Tyrren, or because the Legion seized their businesses, or their families have disappeared. This is a base, it's true. But it's also sort of…a shelter. Anyone who isn't safe in their own village is welcome in this one."

"Not everyone's cut out for secret missions," Orion added. "But everyone who lives here has to help out somehow. Normally I'd be out with a surveillance party of course, but we're required to rotate through all the duty stations on occasion. I just happened to be on the support division's roster today."

Fatima rolled her eyes.

Orion led the way down a stairwell and stood aside at the bottom to hold a door open for the others. Tuesday had been expecting more of the same brightly-lit rooms and polished white floors, but as they filed past Orion to the next stop on the tour, she could not make out much of anything in the dim space beyond.

"Here, take a lantern," Orion instructed. He passed each of them a clear, barely-glowing crystal strung onto a large metal ring. He slipped the ring of his lantern over his arm like a bracelet, leaving the crystal dangling below it. He twisted the crystal in place like he was screwing in a light bulb, and the soft glow intensified until it shone like a flashlight.

"Where are we?" Zed asked as his eyes gradually adjusted to the gloom. The room was cool and humid, quiet but for the occasional echoes of water droplets falling to the ground. He had almost forgotten the entire base was in a cave, but there was no mistaking it now. The rough gray stone of the walls and floor glistened with moisture in the light of the crystal lanterns. Dozens of gigantic cloth sacks that reminded Zed of a boxer's punching bag hung from the ceiling. There was so little space between each one that they had to edge between them single file. Something white and spongy sprouted from the sides of each bag, like tiny ears fanning out to listen in on their conversation.

Tuesday held her crystal up close to examine one. "Are those…?"

"Mushrooms," Fatima said, nodding. "The natural conditions in here are perfect for growing them. We add some of them to the meals served in the dining hall, but mostly they're harvested to be sold in the village market in Kyoto. That, and the crystal mine next door, serve as the main sources of revenue for the base. We try to make most of what we need right here, but there are still a few things we need money to buy from outside sources."

"Makes a good cover for our operations, too," added Orion. "It'd be suspicious if the villagers saw people coming and going around here all the time—kind of a dead giveaway. But since they think we're just employees of the mine heading to work, they pretty much ignore us."

"Wait, why are you telling us all this?" Tuesday asked. "It was one thing for Solomon to bring us in the secret waterfall entrance—he assumed we wouldn't be able to find it again or open the door if we could find it. But you're spilling all the Resistance secrets! Aren't you afraid we'll tell someone? And why do we need to know this stuff anyway?"

They followed Orion back to the door, handing back their lanterns as they passed him.

"Well how are you going to work in these duty stations if you don't know what they're for?" Fatima laughed. "We all have to pitch in somehow, and I don't think you're ideal candidates to send out on missions, what with the Legion looking for you and all."

"You won't be doing any crystal mining, of course," Orion added. "Sharp tools and heavy machinery and all that—only adults allowed. Let's tour the gardens next. That's a job that should be more your speed."

Fatima frowned down at Nyx, who was busy licking water droplets off the walls. "Probably better skip the poultry yard though," she told Orion. "The dodos might not mind, they're pretty hard to ruffle. But I'm pretty sure the chickens would lose their heads completely at the sight of a Gabriel Hound."

"Wait, dodos?" Zed interrupted. "As in, the bird kind of dodo? The extinct kind?"

"Extinct?" Fatima raised an eyebrow at him. "Not as many people keep them as they used to…they don't lay eggs every day like chickens do, and the meat's only good for drying out, or stew—too tough for roasting. But I think extinct is a bit of an exaggeration. Doesn't anyone in your village keep a dodo flock?"

"Our…village?" Tuesday was struggling to follow the turn this conversation had taken.

"What village do you come from, anyway?" Orion asked. "My briefing this morning just said your father had left the Legion, and you would be staying at the base since you don't know where—"

Fatima shot him an annoyed glare. "Shush!" she scolded him under her breath. "They've got enough worries; I'm sure they don't want to be reminded of their family! Enough orphans and refugees end up here, I would think you'd have learned to be a bit more sensitive by now!"

Tuesday dropped back to walk with Zed and Nyx as Fatima and Orion carried on ahead.

"Hurry along now," Fatima called over her shoulder. "We still have another stop to make before lunch!"

"They think we're staying!" whispered Zed. "Like, to live here. Forever."

"Not if I can help it," Tuesday muttered back.

"Well how do you expect to get out of here? We need a plan!"

"We haven't had a plan the entire time we've been in Falinnheim," she answered, "and it hasn't stopped us yet!"

Chapter 22

HOW DOES YOUR GARDEN GROW?

Zed wished, more than anything, he'd had his notebook in his pocket when the soldiers broke into his house and started this bizarre adventure. Having all this new information swirling around in his head, instead of on a page where he could sort and inspect and decipher it, was like trying to have a picnic in a sandstorm. It wasn't quite the same, but he tried to visualize a mental list to sort things out.

He was:
1. trapped in a top-secret spy headquarters
2. with people who believed his dog was evil, or at the very least dangerous and unpredictable

3. and assumed his dad was a villain who had abandoned his children

But it was also a:

4. paranormal research lab
5. refugee camp
6. crystal lightbulb mine
7. mushroom farm
8. extinct wildlife preserve

And the tour wasn't even over yet.

All in all, it was shaping up to be his most interesting day in Falinnheim yet. And given the strangeness of this whole adventure, that was really saying something.

Tuesday, on the other hand, was just offended she had been pulled onto this un-amusement park ride at all. Three days ago, she had been a normal kid minding her own business, and now an entire circus of weird had descended on her life unannounced. She didn't know how or why it had happened, but she was determined that one way or another, she was going to get out of here, go home, and finally get a straight answer out of her parents.

But first, she had to tour a garden, apparently.

Orion and Fatima conducted everyone back up the staircase, down yet another corridor, and finally through a set of double doors that swung aside automatically to admit them as they approached. They found their way blocked by another set of double doors, which formed a sort of airlock between them like the ones Zed had seen on spaceships in science fiction movies. Once the doors behind them closed, the second set parted automatically in front of them.

When they ventured into the mushroom cave earlier, they needed lanterns to combat the cool, clammy darkness. As they entered the garden wing now, Tuesday wished she could have a pair of sunglasses instead. The room was almost unnaturally bright, and as warm and humid as a jungle. The rich, musky scent of damp soil mingled with the fresh grassy notes of leafy plants to create an atmosphere that just smelled green, if such a thing were possible. But another scent wafted like an invisible fog over the others—something mossy, muddy, murky…Tuesday was sure she had smelled something similar before, but she just couldn't place it.

"Welcome to the garden wing," said Fatima. She swept her arms out toward the plants surrounding her as though she was introducing Zed and Tuesday to her oldest and dearest friends.

Zed recalled that a business that sold plants was sometimes called a nursery. That made sense, more or less; they raised "baby" plants from seeds until they had grown enough to graduate to larger gardens. This greenhouse, though, was less like a baby's nursery, and more like a plant metropolis. Everywhere he looked, green leaves waved back at him. The leafy tops of plants were peeking out of raised planting boxes on the ground, dripping out of metal troughs hanging from the walls, and leaning out of tiny balconies cut into the skyscraper pillars holding up the glass ceiling. Vines laden with grapes rappelled down the metal cables suspending hanging strawberry beds. Carrots, beets, radishes, potatoes, green beans, and heads of lettuce crowded into wheeled bins parked along the aisles, waiting for their commute to the kitchen.

The blocks of planting boxes alternated with a few bare areas though, where no leaves reached out for the lights above. As Zed approached one for a better look, he realized it was actually a small pond dug into the gravel floor. A school of silvery fish danced in and out of view in the pool's depths. He knelt on the ground and peered in, wondering if he could identify what kind of fish they were.

"Mind you, keep your fingers back now," an unfamiliar voice croaked. "They'll nip at anything that gets into the water."

Zed looked up. Sitting on a stool on the opposite side of the pond was the oldest woman he had ever seen. Her back and shoulders arched permanently forward, as though she carried the weight of her many years of life around with her in an invisible backpack. Her face puckered and sank like a shrunken apple forgotten at the back of the fridge; even her wrinkles had wrinkles. It was no wonder Zed hadn't noticed her before—she was so short that not even the halo of wispy white hair circling her head could be seen over the plants next to the pond. With the knobbly knuckles and skeletal fingers of one hand, she clutched at a thick wooden walking stick, which she leaned on for support even though she was seated. With the other hand, she dipped into a cloth sack propped up against her stool. She scooped a handful of brown pellets out of the sack and flung them into the water. Instantly the surface of the water roiled and burbled like a pot boiling over as the fish snapped at the morsels. The woman looked up at Zed with a creaky smile, then reached back into the sack for another handful.

Tuesday rounded a corner and nearly tripped over Zed's feet sticking out into the aisle. "A fish tank!" she exclaimed. "I knew I recognized that smell—it's just like the fish aisle of the pet store! I used to go look at the goldfish and guppies and bettas while Mom was picking out chew toys for Nyx. But why keep a fishpond in a greenhouse? They've already got separate rooms for tools, crystals, even mushrooms for crying out loud—couldn't they find space for an 'aquarium hall', or someth—"

Tuesday stopped short as she noticed the old woman, who flung another helping of pellets into the pond. Nyx dashed up behind Tuesday, spotted the woman, and then leaped clean over the pond to greet her, sliding as she landed on the loose gravel on the other side.

Fatima and Orion rounded the corner as well. "Obaachan!" Fatima gasped as she noticed Nyx bounding eagerly toward the woman.

"Nyx! Stop!" yelled Zed.

Nyx bounced up, ready to jump onto the woman's lap with her front paws.

"Hey!" Orion shouted.

Tuesday grimaced—it was too late to do anything. That lady was going to be knocked aside like a bowling pin...

The woman didn't even flinch. She calmly staked her walking stick into the gravel right in front of Nyx. The dog skidded to a halt and sat.

The woman leaned forward, so close that their noses nearly touched, and stared Nyx in the eye. Nyx stared back, frozen, for what seemed an eternity. Then she abruptly laid down and rolled onto her back for a belly rub. The woman turned her stick over and gave Nyx's stomach a couple of gentle taps with the handle.

"Obaachan!" Fatima gushed once she started breathing again. "Obaa—I'm so sorry, I didn't know you were here, we should have been more careful—you could have been hurt—"

"No harm done, young lady," she chuckled in reply. "It'll take more than an overgrown pup to take me down." Then she casually returned to feeding the fish as though nothing had happened.

Fatima blinked a little, trying to regain her composure. "Well, uh...as you can see, Obaachan is feeding some of the fish we raise here in the garden wing," she continued, putting her tour guide persona back on. "Their pond water needs to be filtered and changed out regularly, so the pumps are routed to send that water directly to the plants. Some of the planters, like the troughs hanging on the walls, don't even require soil, in fact—the water is supplemented with the exact mix of nutrients the plants need."

"Makes sense to keep them both in the same space," Orion added. "The plants get watered, the ponds get cleaned, and both the fish and the fruits and vegetables head to the kitchens when they're big enough."

A small crowd of gardeners arrived from the far end of the greenhouse to investigate the shouting. Some backed away with widened eyes as they spotted Nyx. Others just stared, their expressions trapped between curiosity and alarm. Zed was amused to see one woman's mouth was actually hanging open.

From somewhere overhead a bell chimed.

"That's lunch," one of the gardeners called to the others. They all filed back toward the entrance doors, giving Nyx a wide berth as they passed. Nyx paid no attention— she was busy lapping up water from the pond.

"Obaachan, can I help you up?" Fatima offered, preemptively placing a hand under the old woman's elbow.

"Don't fret yourself, pigeon," Obaachan answered, patting the top of her walking stick. "That's what old Shin Biter here is for. Besides, I'm still waiting for my lunch date."

"I'm starving! Hope those rolls are still warm; they looked good," Orion commented as he made his way to the doors.

"Not so fast!" Fatima protested. "We still have to return them to their room!

"Sorry," she added, turning to Zed and Tuesday. "We can't exactly bring a Gabriel Hound into a crowded dining hall—people might panic."

"Or get their lunches stolen, more likely," muttered Tuesday.

"We'll have someone bring your lunch to your room," Fatima offered.

"Why don't we eat right here?" Zed suggested, surveying the empty greenhouse.

"Great, that'll save time," Orion agreed. "Their room is way on the other end of the base anyway." He started for the doors again before Fatima could stop him.

"You go get everyone's food, then—we'll wait here!" Fatima called after him.

As Orion reached the doors, another figure approached from the opposite direction. He stopped in his tracks when he realized who it was, then jumped aside to clear the path as the General strode past him.

"G-good afternoon, General, ma'am!" he stuttered. The General said nothing but nodded in his direction without breaking her stride.

"Ah, there you are, Mavra!" said Obaachan. "About time—I thought you might work right through lunch again—you're always working too hard, you know."

The General let out a patient sigh. "Ready then, mother?" she asked, placing a hand under the old woman's elbow as Fatima had done earlier.

"Oh, stop fussing!" Obaachan scolded, waving the General off with an impatient flick of the wrist before hoisting herself to her feet with her cane. "I'm old—I'm not dead!"

Obaachan was barely any taller standing than she had been sitting, Zed noted, as she and the General crunched slowly down the gravel path and out of sight.

Tuesday and Zed found seats on the ledge of a nearby planting box and settled in to wait for Orion to return with their food.

"Is Obaachan really the General's mother?" Tuesday asked Fatima. "I can't imagine the General ever having been a kid! She's just so…you know…all business, all the time."

"She certainly runs a tight ship," Fatima agreed. "But I think she has to, to keep everyone else going. The General commands respect because she gets things done. And you have to keep in mind—she founded the Resistance herself. She's committed to our mission, so naturally she takes that responsibility seriously."

Zed had never considered that. The Legion, the Resistance, Tyrren, the General…they all seemed like these vast, faceless, impersonal forces playing tug-of-war with his fate. In his mind, Falinnheim existed in a bubble; it was called into being the moment Scrimbley brought them there three days ago and would be set aside like a strange dream the moment he returned home again. He had never given thought to what happened before he arrived, when the Resistance was just a struggling band of rebels—or even longer before, when Tyrren hadn't been in power at all. He began to see that each of these people had their own stories, their own histories, their own motivations and fears, worries and hopes.

"What do you know about the founding of the Resistance?" he asked Fatima. "How did the General and Solomon and everyone get involved?"

Fatima smiled—a small, sad smile. She no longer seemed like the confident, efficient tour guide she had been portraying all morning—more like someone hearing an old song on the radio or thumbing through a dusty photo album.

"I'm too young to remember much of what life was like before Tyrren took over. Just little snippets are all I can offer from personal experience. I have a vague memory of seeing the Moderator and a few other members of the royal family once, from the crowd at some sort of official event in Alexandria. I remember it was cold—maybe it was a Solstice celebration? Anyway, I was only eight when my mother was taken away by Tyrren's guards, a couple of years after he took power. I don't even know why they took her. After that, it was like she had just never existed at all, as far as the officials were concerned. My father suspected they'd be coming back for us before long, so he made contact with a couple of Resistance agents and brought my brother and me here with him. We've lived here ever since. The base has been expanded and renovated in that time, and of course many more people have joined the Resistance over the years, but that's all I know about it for sure."

"Wow. I'm sorry…" said Zed quietly.

"Surely you've heard rumors, though?" Tuesday coaxed. "About how the Resistance got started?"

"A few," Fatima admitted. "People say the General decided to start the Resistance after her family was killed on the day of the revolution. I think her husband and son had jobs in the palace, of some sort. They were killed along with the royal family during Tyrren's takeover. The General knew Tyrren's people would be coming for anyone connected to those killed in the siege, so they wouldn't talk—they planned to sweep the whole thing under the rug like everyone wanted Tyrren to be in charge all along—so she and Obaachan left their home in Kyoto and went into hiding in the mountains. I'm not sure how she got involved with Captain Solomon and the other leaders, but somehow they gradually gathered up enough supplies to transform an abandoned mine into the base as you see it today."

"How long ago was that?" Zed asked.

"Sixteen years," said Fatima grimly. "I still have hope, though—progress may be slow, but someday we'll get rid of Tyrren once and for all."

Orion returned with a tray of food: steaming bowls of the soup they had seen the kitchen staff working on earlier, a large bottle of apple cider, and a basket of rolls. Nyx darted over to investigate, her snout and paws caked in moist dirt—apparently she had started digging a hole in one of the planting boxes when no one was looking. Orion tossed her a roll, which she snatched in the air and chomped down in a matter of seconds.

As Zed tucked into his lunch he added to his mental list:

> 9. hydroponic greenhouse
> 10. indoor fish farm

It just seemed right to finish the list off, once he had started it, but he no longer found it very useful in organizing his swirling thoughts. He was no longer so concerned with what the Resistance base was, or how he and Tuesday fit into their plans. Zed realized now that this was much, much bigger than either of them.

Chapter 23

ROOTS

Things loosened up for Tuesday and Zed after that, but not by much. As they were no longer suspected of being spies and had delivered the General all the explanations she'd demanded, they were no longer locked in their room during their free time between duty stations. Solomon even presented them with a gift: a doorknob, which attached to the inside of their door magnetically so they wouldn't need a guard to open it for them from the outside. They remained in the same room, however—Orion explained that for some reason, none of the other Resistance members were very keen to have a Gabriel Hound with them in the shared dormitories—and Tuesday was unwilling to dismiss the fact that their room was designed as a holding cell, not a guest room. Zed agreed with her, at least, that the idea of their conversations still being monitored was not outside the realm of possibility. This left them with a very interesting dilemma: they had a lot of things they desperately wanted to discuss but could only do so away from the privacy of their room. In other words, in public.

How could they hold a private conversation surrounded by other people? At school, this could be accomplished by the stealthy passing of written notes, but they didn't have access to paper or pencils. And as they didn't really know their way around the base's maze of corridors they were always escorted to their duty stations, so a whispered conference in the hallways was out of the question. They weren't allowed to leave Nyx alone, nor was she welcome in the dining hall, so they didn't have the noise of a crowd to cover their discussion. They had, however, managed to convince each of their daily escorts to allow them to eat in the garden wing, rather than returning to their room for meals. Zed and Tuesday alternated meals— one of them filled a tray in the dining hall with enough food to share, while the other waited in the greenhouse with Nyx.

This arrangement continued for four days. Each morning, as the artificial sunrise in their room signaled the start of the day, Zed and Tuesday would wait for that day's escort to take them to the greenhouse for breakfast. Their guides were always paired, but it was never the same partnership twice—although they did get Fatima again once, paired with one of the women they had noticed in the repair bay on their first tour of the base. Each day they worked in one of the support division's duty stations, tutored in each task by their chaperones, and then returned to their room after dinner so they could prepare to start the whole cycle over again. Tuesday had actually taken to keeping a tally of each day they spent at the base by wiping a finger in the corner of their bathroom mirror after her shower every evening—this way, her marks only showed when the room was steamed up with fog and disappeared as soon as the bathroom door opened again. She knew there was no reason to conceal the marks, and that no one would care even if they did discover them; there was just something comforting about having control over a secret list, since she had lost control of any other aspect of her life.

"It's been a week since we left home," Tuesday commented to Zed when she emerged from the bathroom the evening she marked her fifth stripe in the corner of the mirror. "It was a Wednesday, when—" She caught herself before she could say anything revealing. Tuesday eyed the ceiling with suspicion, as though the unseen guard she assumed to be listening hovered over their conversation literally, instead of just figuratively.

"When we met Scrimbley," Zed finished for her. The General already knew that part, after all.

Zed pondered on what had become of their home in the past week. What had the soldiers done after Nyx held them off? Did they wait around, hoping Mom and Dad would return? Or had they run off, thinking the struggle had already attracted too much attention? Mrs. Alvarez had surely come over to check on them before long, wondering where they were…and would have called the police, after she saw the destruction left by Nyx's battle with the soldiers. Everyone probably thought he and Tuesday had been kidnapped or something—which, come to think of it, wasn't so far from the truth. He just hoped Mrs. Alvarez was all right. He shuddered to think what might have happened if she had arrived while the soldiers were still there.

This speculation was useless though, Zed decided. There was no way to guess how events had unfolded in their absence, because it all hinged on where their parents had really gone on that morning one week ago. And wherever it was, obviously, the trip had not gone according to plan.

"Do you think…" Zed stopped. He wanted to choose his words carefully. "Do you think anyone would mind if we spent some more time in the greenhouse before bed? I'd just like to relax—somewhere other than our room for once."

Tuesday craned her neck up at the ceiling in reply, as though asking the unseen guard for permission. Nothing happened.

"I don't hear any objections!" she said with a mischievous grin. "Come on, Nyx!"

They made a few wrong turns and had to ask a couple of people they passed in the halls to point them in the right direction again, but they made it to the garden wing's doors without too much trouble.

"I think I'm actually starting to get the hang of this place!" Tuesday congratulated herself. "Maybe next time we run into Solomon we could ask him to let up on the constant supervision thing."

The greenhouse was quiet but for the sound of their footsteps crunching along the gravel path. In the near-silence of their surroundings they unconsciously lowered their conversation to a whisper. They sat on the ledge of a planting box next to one of the ponds and gazed at the fish for a while, hypnotized by their graceful, fluid dance. The cheerful trickling of the irrigation system was so soothing that Zed thought he might fall asleep, if the lights weren't so bright. The warm, moist air of the greenhouse wrapped itself around him like a blanket.

Suddenly Nyx, who had been peering with curiosity down at the fish flickering in and out of view in the pond, stood at attention. Her ears perked up. Tuesday didn't even have time to finish asking, "Nyx, what do you—" before the dog bounded along the path and disappeared behind the leafy curtain of green screening their view.

"We must not be alone after all," said Zed.

When they caught up with Nyx, they found her sitting next to a raised garden bed, her tongue lolling out happily as a pair of hands rubbed her ears. They were relieved that her sudden entrance had not alarmed anyone, and that she did not appear to have knocked anyone over in her exuberance, until they came close enough to realize who the hands belonged to.

The General was kneeling next to a bed of melons, her fingernails caked in black soil, petting Nyx. She looked up at Zed and Tuesday standing over her with dumbfounded expressions and bestowed a rare smile—just a small, wry grin tugging at one corner of her mouth, but still, a smile.

"Looks like my secret hideout has been found out," she said.

"What are…why—" Tuesday spluttered. "I mean, I just didn't expect to see you, here, doing gardening work—"

"You think I should leave the manual labor to other people?" the General asked.

"When Orion mentioned everyone was required to rotate through all the duty stations, I didn't really think he meant you," said Zed.

"I prefer to come after the official work shifts are over to wind down a bit and sort out my thoughts, but yes, generals can pull weeds too. I so rarely leave the base that I rather get to missing leaves and water and dirt."

The General released Nyx's ears and plunged her hands back into the crumbly soil to dig out a sprout that didn't belong. She wrenched it out and tapped it against the side of the planting bed to release the extra dirt caught in the trailing roots.

"Can I ask you a question?" Zed ventured after a moment of hesitation.

"I suppose."

"When you came to get your mother, on the first day we were touring the support division—"

"Obaachan?" the General interrupted.

Zed nodded.

"Obaachan isn't my mother."

"But when you came to get her for lunch, you said—"

The General sighed. "It is traditional, at least in my village, to treat all elder relatives with a parental level of respect. 'Obaachan' isn't even her name, it just means 'Grandma'. Everyone at the base has adopted her as a sort of mascot. As she is by far the oldest person living here, in a way, she's everyone's grandmother." There was a long pause before the General continued speaking, as though she was weighing whether to continue at all. "Obaachan is actually my mother-in-law…she was my husband's mother."

"I'm sorry," said Zed. "Fatima mentioned your family had all been killed."

"What happened?" Tuesday asked.

Zed winced—he thought Tuesday's curiosity was far too blunt—but if the General thought so, she didn't show it.

"My husband was the Captain of the Royal Guard," she explained, "the Moderator's personal protector. As far as I've been able to piece together, Tyrren managed to draw enough of the lower-ranking guards over to his side—secretly of course—that on the day his forces raided the palace, those that remained loyal to the Regents Council were overpowered. My husband was killed defending the Moderator. He and our son—he had only been promoted to the Royal Guard a couple of years earlier, but he was so proud to follow in his father's profession—they refused to retreat from their oath to defend the royal family with their lives."

Zed and Tuesday had no idea what to say in the face of such a tragic story, so they just didn't. The silence that followed was not tense or awkward, however; it was a moment of comfortable reverence, an invitation for memory to take a seat among them and have its say, and no one felt compelled to interrupt.

At length the sound of approaching footsteps signaled an end to their conference. A man in a dusty black cloak and mud-caked boots swept past their shield of leaves.

"General—" he said shortly, with a bow, "—the report on our mission to New Angkor." He handed the General a stack of papers, along with a small glass sphere, and retreated with another bow.

The General nodded. She read the report, her eyes sliding back and forth, scanning the lines of text with mechanical efficiency. At length she set the pages down with a sigh.

"Well, it wasn't easy, but a team of agents was able to make contact with Scrimbley," she summarized.

"And?" Tuesday asked. "What did he say? Did he tell them anything about the transporting device, or the soldiers who attacked us?"

The General shook her head. "The agents told him we had recovered you children, and wanted more information on how you got here, and why. They offered him a considerable amount of money to cooperate—he's been a resource we've called on a few times before, and he's always been helpful, for the right price. He said—well, I suppose we should just watch the interview."

The General held the sphere out in her palm to give Tuesday and Zed a better look. Zed recalled Fatima using one just like it the first time they met. The General pressed a fingertip to the surface of the ball and swirled it clockwise around the circumference. Scrimbley's face appeared, like a floating head in a crystal ball Tuesday had seen imitated once at a Halloween party, and began to speak:

"I ain't sayin' nuthin—not worth it. Ain't nuthin you can offer that's worth upsetting him."

"Who do you mean?" asked the voice of someone out of view. "The children's father?"

Scrimbley continued: "You best take care you don't upset him neither. I don't care who comes after me—you lot, the soldiers, or the Liberator himself—their father's the only one I'd be feared of running afoul of."

Scrimbley's face dissolved into a dark mist, which gradually dissipated until the sphere was silent and transparent once more.

The General sighed again. "I'm sure this must be upsetting to you. We didn't get much in the way of answers, but one thing is clear—your father is definitely involved in something here in Falinnheim. I know you were hoping to find out more about the rhymes you recovered, but for your own safety, I must ask you to reconsider. The Legion is not to be trifled with."

Now the silence was awkward. The General put the ball into a pocket of her robes. "You know, I don't believe you actually got to ask your question, earlier," she commented to Zed to break the tension.

"I've got two questions, actually," he replied.

"All right…"

"Why do people call you the Green Fly?"

"Oh, that. More of a joke that got out of hand than anything, really. Tyrren has no idea who's behind the Resistance, but he desperately wants the public to view it as a lawless disruption to society. A couple of years ago he had the Information Ministry display posters in every village that showed him swatting a bug representing the Resistance. But it didn't work out like he hoped—rather than seeing the Resistance as a minor irritation to be squashed, people took the poster to mean that the Resistance was vexing him and he was unable to keep it under control, just as a fly might avoid being swatted. The Information Ministry took the posters down right away, but since the name had already stuck they decided to just go with it—they applied it as a nickname for the leader of the Resistance, whoever it might be. Our surveillance agents thought this was amusing and started using the term inside the base as well."

As the General spoke, Tuesday sat down on the edge of the planting bed where the General had set down the report papers. Noiselessly, she slid the top page off of the stack and slipped it under her cloak.

"What was the other question?" the General asked Zed.

"Fatima mentioned you and Obaachan lived in Kyoto before Tyrren took over. You said your husband led the Royal Guards. I was wondering—what was your job? What did you do before everything changed, before the Resistance?"

There was that smile again—just a small, thoughtful grin, pulled off to one side, as though it was trying to sneak off of her face before anyone noticed it.

"I used to be a florist, actually."

Chapter 24

AT LAST, A PLAN

Zed and Tuesday were relieved when the lights in the greenhouse dimmed and the General dismissed them back to their room. Zed was anxious for some time alone with his thoughts, a chance to wade into the pool of new information sloshing around in his brain and try to make some sense of it. Tuesday was anxious for an entirely different reason—a reason that was not revealed to Zed until they trekked back to their living quarters.

The moment the door clicked shut, Tuesday put a silencing finger to her lips, pointing up at the ceiling with the other hand. Then, trying to dampen any crinkling sounds as much as possible, she drew the stolen page of the General's report from her cloak.

Zed's mouth fell open as he mimed her a disapproving glare. He was caught between feeling impressed with her daring and appalled at her reckless and, well—less than honest approach to intelligence gathering. He was not appalled enough to resist reading it, however.

Departmental Daily Summary
Medical
-Daily patient report: one smashed thumbnail, one dizzy spell, one twisted ankle, and one juvenile with loose tooth—all treated and released.
-No patients presently admitted for overnight monitoring.
-Market requisition form for disinfectant concentrate, hellebore extract, butterfly milk, and star willow buds enclosed.

Operations
-New missing persons flyers in Alexandria, Etrusia, and Olympus Minor—copies enclosed.
-Rhyming coded message found in Kyoto market—copy enclosed.
-New campaign to launch in West Thebes on Friday. Expansion to Etrusia by Bounty 46th if successful.
-Palace agent weekly reports enclosed.

Research

Conclusion: limited benefit of sending Gabriel Hound on missions outweighed by risk potential, unless true master can be located. Draws too much attention for covert operations. Theoretical potential to host a new pack if unbroken hounds could be located and broken.

Security

-Responded to report of disturbance in Men's Dormitory 3. Basket of dental beads had been tied to the doorknob—when cleaning pods entered, the basket tipped over and spilled dental beads onto water puddle on the floor, causing them all to foam up at once. Pods were trapped in the suds. Sent pods to repair bay. No suspects at this time—investigation continues. Incident report filed with dormitory supervisor, copy enclosed.

-Repair requested for faulty code panel at mine exit tunnel. Service request form sent to support division head, copy enclosed.

Support

-Grain provision levels adequate.

-Market requisition form for salt, paper, cheese, thread, and dental beads enclosed.

-Quarterly mushroom harvest complete, shipment to Kyoto market at sunrise.
-Maintenance crew located leak in geothermal pipe—repaired.
-Morale officers meeting to plan Equinox festival scheduled for the Bounty 34th dinner break.

In sequence, Tuesday pointed to lines under the Operations, Support, and Security headings. She put a finger to her lips again and motioned to Zed to follow her to the bathroom. She turned the shower on and closed the bathroom door. When the air in the room was sufficiently steamy, she dragged her finger through the condensation clouding the mirror's surface and wrote one word:

TONIGHT.

Zed nodded, then wiped the mirror clean with his sleeve. He was pretty sure he understood Tuesday's plan. It would probably even work. He just wasn't sure it was a good idea.

Zed jolted awake. It was still dark. He had known he would not be able to stay awake all night, and that their plan was much more likely to succeed in the latter half of the night, but as they had no way of keeping track of time their only option had been to head for bed as usual and put their plan into action the first time either of them happened to wake up. He scooted off of his bedroll and shook Tuesday's shoulder. Normally waking Tuesday up was an activity to be approached with extreme caution, but naturally this time was different—it was her plan, after all.

Tuesday sat up, slipped on her shoes, and fumbled in the darkness toward the door. She turned the knob and eased the door open as silently as she could manage. Nyx stretched and yawned in the sliver of light intruding from the hallway, then followed Zed and Tuesday out of the room.

The corridor was still lit, although not quite at the intensity Zed and Tuesday were accustomed to in the daytime. Thankfully, it was also deserted.

"We need to find the crystal mine," Tuesday whispered. "The security controls on the exit door are broken—we'll be able to slip right out."

"Any idea where the mine is?" asked Zed.

"No, but we'll figure it out. It's supposed to be near the mushroom cave, and we already know where that is."

This statement was accurate in that they had visited the mushroom growing area before. There is a difference, however, in being familiar with a destination, and in knowing the route to get there from somewhere else. They decided to retrace the path they had followed with Orion and Fatima on their first day in the support division, starting at the dining hall. They passed a couple of bleary-eyed workers pulling on aprons—probably heading to the kitchens to get an early start on breakfast preparations,

Zed theorized—but no one took much notice of them. When they located the entrance doors to the dining hall, they knew that the door to the left was the repair bay, and the mushroom cave was at the bottom of the stairs at the end of the corridor.

Zed paused at the top of the stairs. "We don't have to go through with this, you know," he whispered to Tuesday. "The General has a copy of the new message they found in Kyoto. She'll probably want us to translate it for her—we won't even have to do anything sneaky to read it. It's not too late to call the whole thing off and head back to our room."

"Okay, let's say we did that," Tuesday huffed. "The General shows us the message—and then what? We're stuck here while she gets to track down whoever's sending the messages? She's not interested in helping us—she's only helping herself!"

"I want to figure out who's sending the messages as much as you do!" Zed retorted. "But that doesn't mean we have to leap at the first hint of a way out of here. The Legion is out there looking for us, and for Dad. We definitely won't get any answers if we get captured!"

"I'm not afraid of them!" Tuesday scowled and folded her arms.

"It's not about being afraid. I just want to make sure we're being smart about this. We don't know what we're getting ourselves into. It's just not…safe."

"You're right," Tuesday said, "it's not safe. We don't know whose clues we're following. We don't have any food or money to take with us. We don't know how to get to Kyoto, or what we'll find when we get there—"

"Wow, you're really convincing me here," Zed interrupted.

"—but the alternative is to just hide here forever," Tuesday continued. "Nothing worth doing is ever really safe."

Zed let out a resigned sigh. Somehow, he had already known Tuesday would get her way, but at least in persuading him she had to justify her reasoning. "If this all goes horribly wrong," he said with a weak smile, "I'm blaming you, okay?"

The sound of Nyx's toenails clacking against the polished floors echoed through the stairwell as they made their way to the mushroom cave. There were three doors on this landing—three identical, unmarked doors. Zed and Tuesday knew the first led to the mushroom cave, but they had no idea what lay behind the others. Tuesday tried the second door, but found it locked. She was just reaching for the knob on the third when—

"Hey! What are you doing there?"

A woman in long brown robes had just emerged from the mushroom room, a crystal lantern still dangling from her wrist.

"We…uhh…" Zed's mind went blank.

Tuesday slapped on her perkiest smile. "Oh, sorry, we're looking for the mushroom cave—we're supposed to help pack a shipment for the market before sunrise. Is this not it?"

"About time you showed up," the woman complained. "My shift's ending, and we're never going to get that shipment packed in time if we're shorthanded! This door is the mushroom cave. Now, I'm off to get some sleep. Here's a lantern," she added, slipping the glowing shard off of her arm and forcing it into Zed's hand. "Go in and report to Theseus, in the green tunic—he'll get you up to speed."

"Thank you, we'll do that!" Tuesday responded cheerily.

As soon as the woman's footsteps on the stairs faded, Tuesday allowed the chipper expression to melt off her face. "Right then, where were we?" she said to herself as she tried the third door.

The knob turned. As she had hoped, Tuesday found herself staring into a tunnel lined with crystals. Zed had imagined the crystals might glow all on their own, but the glassy shards jutting out from the tunnel walls didn't provide any illumination as they cautiously ventured in; they had to huddle in the puddle of light provided by their lantern, occasionally tripping over one another's feet. They passed cavernous cathedrals and narrow, squeezing alcoves, serpentine passes and arrow-straight aisles, all bored into the rock as minerals had been cleared away from the mine over time. At Zed's insistence, they resisted the urge to explore these side paths and kept instead to the widest and most direct central vein, which sloped gradually downward as it led them further and further from the heart of the base. After what seemed an eternity their lantern at last shone on a most welcome sight: there was a door up ahead.

"This must be the exit!" Tuesday whispered. "The control panel is supposed to be broken, so we shouldn't need a security code to get out."

They approached the door—a massive, perfectly smooth stone slab set into the jagged cave wall. As Tuesday had predicted, there was an illuminated panel set into the wall to the right of the door. She confidently jabbed a finger into the center of the glowing pad.

Nothing happened.

She tried to force her fingertips into the seam at the side of the door, hoping to pry it forward, or slide it to one side.

Nothing happened.

"Open—up—stupid—door!" she muttered, pressing her palms flat against the slab and leaning in with her shoulder.

"By 'broken', they must have meant 'stuck closed', not that they couldn't lock it," Zed observed unnecessarily.

"Well now what are we supposed to do?" Tuesday grumbled.

Nyx padded up to Tuesday's side and sniffed at the base of the wall, then pressed her nose into the seam of the door. Her eyes glowed blue for just a moment, reflecting off of the polished stone slab in front of her. The door popped open and slid into the rockface to the left, exactly like an elevator door. Unlike an elevator door, however, it did not roll gradually aside, being pulled to the left by something mechanical—it was more like the door was pushed away by a force on the right.

"Hmm…the lock must be magnetic," Zed theorized, by now accustomed to his dog's growing resume of supernatural abilities. "Looks like Nyx was able to reverse the direction of the magnetic field."

They peered out at their first view of the outside world in days. The door opened directly onto a rocky slope, dotted here and there with the few scraggly evergreen trees that had managed to elbow their way out from between the flat, crumbly stones. It was still dark, but a half-hearted kind of darkness that hinted the sun was beginning to think about peeping over the horizon. Nyx darted out from between Zed and Tuesday and galloped down the slope, sliding along from one wave of loose, shifting pebbles to the next like a surfer. Tuesday and Zed had much slower going, picking their way down the slope in the feeble glow of their lantern, charting whichever path seemed the least steep between trees, clinging to each one as they arrived to keep from sliding to the bottom in a gravel avalanche.

The edges of the world were just beginning to bleed the faintest pink into the sky when they finally met up with Nyx at the base of the slope. She stood in the middle of a wide dirt path, sniffing at a metal pole. A bent, rusty arrow at the top pointed drunkenly down the path away from the slope. Tuesday took the lantern from Zed and held it over her head. She could just make out the weathered engraving: KYOTO, ¼ LEAGUE.

"Excellent," she declared, "we should get there well before sunrise. See, I knew this would work out!"

"We need to hurry up," Zed warned. "Remember, the mushroom shipment is leaving the base at sunrise. We don't want to run into anyone we know at the market."

"No problem. We'll just poke around the market, find this message, and be on our way before anyone realizes we're not in our beds."

"On our way where?"

Tuesday dismissed Zed's concern with an impatient wave. "Oh, you know…wherever the message says. We'll figure it out. Don't get ahead of yourself."

The message turned out to be easy enough to find. When they reached the empty market square at the heart of the village, they found a bulletin board similar to the one in New Angkor. Tacked on the back side was a stack of identical papers, tucked between the curling, warped pages of advertisements for a noodle delivery service and a kite festival. Tuesday ripped off the top page. Zed held the lantern up and peered over her shoulder to read:

> HIGGLEDY PIGGLEDY, EEL LIVER PIE,
> THE SUN'S IN YOUR POCKET, THE MOON'S IN
>   YOUR EYE.
> WHEN THE STARS COME OUT TO SING
> WRAP THEM ALL UP IN YOUR GOLDEN
>   STRING.

Tuesday was rarely at a loss for words, but this development knocked the air right out of her lungs.

"I don't understand…" Zed wracked his brain, grasping at any strand of logic that might explain the clue, some cognitive leap he was missing. "That's not a nursery rhyme I've ever heard before. And even if it was, I can't find any combination of words that would give us instructions to follow…"

"It's…a fake…" Tuesday realized. She started as this information passed through her like an electric shock. She dropped the page and grabbed Zed's arm. "We need to get out of here. Now."

"Why? What's going on?" asked Zed in alarm.

"This is a trap."

They turned around to look for Nyx, who had run off again—and bumped right into a man who had come up behind them. A man wearing an orange tunic, covered by a vest of black scaled armor.

Chapter 25

GLOVES AND UMBRELLAS

"You're up awfully early," the young soldier observed, staring down at Zed and Tuesday. "Where are your parents?"

Zed noted the irony in this question; the question everyone in Fallinnheim seemed to have for them was the one they had absolutely no way to answer. Something else caught Tuesday's attention, however—a single word.

"Parents?" she repeated. Most people had been interested in their father, specifically, up to this point.

"You shouldn't be wandering alone in the dark," the soldier said. "Where do you live? I can escort you home."

Tuesday could have laughed out loud in relief. He didn't know! If Nyx stayed out of sight, they might be able to talk their way out of this!

"We're…uh…visiting from out of town," Tuesday explained (truthfully, more or less.)

"Well, who did you come with?"

"We're just waiting for the market to open—thank you so much for your concern, but we'll be fine!" Tuesday grabbed Zed's arm and steered him in the opposite direction.

"Not so fast!" The soldier stepped in front of Tuesday, blocking her path. "I can't just leave you out here alone. Are you meeting someone at the market? The vendors should be arriving to set up any time now."

The market! Maybe they could convince whoever brought the mushroom shipment down from the base to claim them without giving too much away…

Tuesday's hopes for a smooth exit were dashed as an older soldier arrived. A soldier that looked…familiar.

"What's going on here?" he asked.

"Oh, there you are, Nicodemus! Found a couple of unsupervised children," the first soldier explained.

Nicodemus pulled a lantern of his own out of his cloak pocket. He held it up to Zed's face, and then Tuesday's. As he leaned close to inspect them, his hot breath puffing steam into the chilly morning air, Tuesday remembered where she'd seen the man before, and her heart plummeted into her stomach. He had been leading the group of soldiers that stayed behind to capture them on the road to Kyoto. His face crinkled into a satisfied smirk as he recognized them, too.

"These two are wanted fugitives, Leander," Nicodemus announced. "We need to take them to Alexandria immediately."

"Fugitives?" The first soldier sounded incredulous. "You mean runaways?"

"I mean fugitives," Nicodemus growled.

"That's ridiculous, they're just children! What could they possibly be wanted for?"

"You would do well to listen to your partner, officer." This was a new voice, a dry, smooth, level voice, almost hypnotic in its even, expressionless tone. Zed and Tuesday strained to see over Leander's shoulder as two more men emerged from the shadows. The soldiers whipped around. Nicodemus's hand jumped instinctively to the silver rod fastened at his hip.

"We'll take them from here," said the man on the right. It was not an order, but a simple statement of fact, as though he had every confidence the soldiers would defer to his wishes.

"I don't—" Leander began to protest. He swallowed the rest of his words as the men pulled official-looking red seals out of their cloaks in unison. The men did not appear to be wearing any sort of uniform; their clothes did not match, they wore no armor or badges, as the Legion did, and were not carrying any visible weapons. And yet the appearance of those seals stopped Leander and Nicodemus cold.

Nicodemus grimaced, but bowed deeply, his face unable to match the decorum of his posture. "Of course," he said through gritted teeth. "Anything for the Red Hand."

Leander glanced uncertainly over at his partner but bowed as well.

Again, in unison, the men returned the seals to their cloaks. They each extended a hand toward Zed and Tuesday, as though they expected them to grab ahold and come along willingly.

"Fat chance!" Tuesday spat. "You really think we'd agree to go anywhere with you?"

"It is not necessary for you to agree," said the man on the left in the same hypnotic drone. He tugged a close-fitting leather glove onto one hand. His partner circled around, cutting between the children and the soldiers as he did the same.

"Run for it!" Tuesday screamed. She dove between the men, sliding in the dirt with one leg outstretched like a baseball player stealing home base. Zed scrambled in the opposite direction and ducked under the second man's arm. For one instant he thought he might have made it but looked back when he felt something grab his ankle. A gloved hand closed around his leg—on his bare skin, underneath the leg of his jeans—and held fast. The man did not tug him backward or make any effort to grab him with his other, ungloved hand; he just crouched there, calmly gripping Zed's ankle, his face an expressionless mask.

Zed tried to kick out of the man's grasp, but his leg wouldn't move. It felt cold for an instant, then a bit tingly—and then had no feeling at all. Zed searched wildly for Tuesday and saw that the other man had her by the arm, which hung limp from his gloved fist. Tuesday spun on her back and kicked at the glove with her shoe; the man released her arm and reached toward her face as she scooted backwards, crablike, in the dust.

"Don't let him cover—" was all time Zed had to say before a glove clamped over his mouth. His vision blurred. Tuesday screamed—a scream that sounded to Zed like it was coming from underwater—

The hand abruptly released him. All Zed could see, as his surroundings swam back into view, was that everything was suddenly bright blue. Bright, and warm, for some reason. A dark shadow moved in front of him, blocking the flickering glare.

His eyes slowly slid back into focus. Zed found himself sprawled in the dust next to Tuesday, surrounded by a wall of electric blue flames. And in front of them, crouching behind the open canopy of an umbrella, was their father.

"Can you walk?" he asked Zed shortly, his back still turned to them.

Zed felt his ankle. Still a bit tingly, but the feeling was starting to return.

He didn't wait for an answer. "Go with Nyx—now, no arguments."

Tuesday hoisted Zed onto his good leg with her one working arm. As they hobbled to the edge of the square, the wall of flame moved with them, parting momentarily around their father before closing again behind him. They shuffled to a nearby building and stumped up the wooden staircase to its balcony, Tuesday half-dragging Zed as he hopped along. Nyx crouched at the base of the stairs; the ring of flames had disappeared, leaving only the fire engulfing her body as she snarled in the direction of the two Red Hand agents staring impassively at her from the edge of the square. In one synchronous glance, the agents looked up at Tuesday and Zed on the balcony. They looked back at Nyx once more, nodded to each other, then turned and disappeared into the shadows of the nearest alley.

Zed sank to the floor of the balcony beside Tuesday, who stepped up to the railing and scanned the square below. The gradually rising sun cast long shadows onto the figures circling and prowling in a watchful dance: the two soldiers, each holding long swords at the ready, faced their father, still brandishing his opened umbrella like a shield.

"I was hoping to be the one to find you, Beren," Nicodemus snarled. "Leander—leave us," he called to his partner, without looking at him. "I have unfinished business with this vermin."

"What's going on?" Leander protested. "Is—is that a Gabriel Hound? And the Red Hand—I thought they were a myth!"

"They don't teach you everything in apprenticeship, boy; consider this your real graduation. Last chance—go now, before I take you out myself!"

"I am not your apprentice—I'm your partner, and I'm not going anywhere!"

Nicodemus's sword clashed against Leander's; in one swift motion he twisted it from Leander's grasp. As he did so, it transformed back into a plain silver rod.

Mr. Furst took advantage of their momentary inattention to cut between the soldiers, forcing the disarmed junior officer away from his partner as he charged Nicodemus with his umbrella and pushed him off balance. Zed winced, expecting the sword to tear right through the umbrella, but was amazed to hear a metallic clang when they collided.

Instantly the umbrella transformed into, of all things, an ordinary chair. Mr. Furst grabbed it by the backrest and thrust the chair legs at Nicodemus's sword, then gave a sharp twist. The sword was almost wrenched from Nicodemus's hand; the extra rod fell from his grasp as he struggled to maintain his grip on his own weapon. The sword shrank away and became a circular shield, studded with spikes. The chair turned into a shepherd's crook, which hooked around the edge of the shield, which changed into a spear. Axe, club, dagger, staff—the weapons transformed as quickly as Tuesday and Zed could identify them, swinging and striking and bashing and clanging in a violent silver whirlwind.

Tuesday caught a flicker of movement at the corner of her vision. She tore her eyes away from her father just in time to see Nyx dart aside to allow someone up the stairs. Zed struggled to his feet, and Tuesday jumped in front of him to face the intruder sprinting up the steps to the landing.

It was their mother.

"Mom!" Zed and Tuesday gasped. Their mother swept them into a hug, the voluminous folds of her cloak draping over their shoulders like a warm blanket.

"I'm so proud of you!" she gushed. "You did so well, all on your own! There's so much to explain, but I'm afraid it will have to wait—Nyx and I have work to do."

She stepped up to the railing and surveyed the battle below. Instantly, Nyx sprang from her post and launched herself toward the dueling pair.

Mr. Furst held a shining, snakelike whip; with a single flick forward, it coiled around Nicodemus's arm. One yank sent the soldier stumbling to his knees. The whip transformed into a baseball bat; Mr. Furst lunged forward, stepping into his swing, the bat slicing through the air to connect with his opponent—

The bat swung clean over Nicodemus. It flew from

Mr. Furst's grip and landed in a cloud of dust halfway across the square, once more in the form of an umbrella.

Tuesday's insides knotted as a sickening cry pierced the air. The sound seemed to stab into her heart, slashing her to the core. For a fleeting instant she imagined that such an unearthly noise could only have come from Nyx, but one glance at the square below showed it was not the dog at all—it was her father.

Mr. Furst fell backward and clutched at his boot, sucking in quick, ragged breaths through clenched teeth. Leander stood over him gripping the sledgehammer he had just used to smash Mr. Furst's foot. The hammer then became a spear, which Leander pointed directly at Mr. Furst's heart. Behind him Nicodemus scrambled to his feet, clutching a monstrous curved saber and steaming with rage.

"I told you this is my battle!" Nicodemus seethed.

"I don't care about some personal feud—I won't abandon my partner!" Leander retorted. "Let's take him back to headquarters and let them sort this out."

"I'm not about to let those fools at headquarters steal my vengeance!" Nicodemus bellowed, tugging at the spear.

They were so busy arguing they never even knew what hit them.

Chapter 26

ESCAPES AND REUNIONS

The soldiers collapsed against each other and folded to the ground like shuffled cards. Nyx's teeth were still clamped around the end of Leander's spear. She extinguished herself and leaped over the unconscious heap to give Mr. Furst's face a celebratory slurp.

"Well, I've done what I can," said Mrs. Furst grimly. "Tuesday, hurry down there and get Dad his umbrella—Zed and I will catch up."

"What…did you do, exactly?" Zed asked while his mother helped him down the stairs. He tried to phrase this as politely as possible, but he wasn't sure what she had been able to accomplish this far from the conflict.

"Well, I admit it probably won't last long, but that electric shock has the soldiers knocked out for now—hopefully it will buy us a few minutes to make our escape."

"But Nyx did that," he pointed out.

Mrs. Furst wasn't really listening. They hobbled across the square to join Nyx and Mr. Furst.

"I thought I told you to stay at the safe house!" Mr. Furst laughed through gritted teeth as his wife knelt to help ease his injured foot out of his boot.

"Well luckily for you, I don't take orders very well," she answered with a worried smile.

Tuesday handed her father his umbrella, which changed into a crutch the moment he touched it. "Don't worry, I'll be fine," he assured them. Wincing, he stood and tucked the crutch under his arm. "We need to get going. There's no telling how long they'll be out, and people will be arriving any minute to set up the market."

As if summoned by his words, at that moment a man appeared at the opposite side of the square. Tuesday gasped in alarm, but Zed put a restraining hand on her arm and pointed down at Nyx. Her tail was wagging.

"Someone you know?" their mother asked. "Nyx says he's okay."

Zed wasn't sure what that meant, but as a ray of sunlight illuminated the man's face, he and Tuesday realized Nyx was right.

It was Solomon.

Solomon ran over to a large bell mounted on a pole near the bulletin board. He yanked the rope and shouted over the bell's calls: "Help! Someone has attacked the village patrol!"

"What is he doing?" Tuesday said as she helped Zed limp away from the exposed clearing. "He's going to get us caught!"

Zed grinned. "No, he's not. He just found us a way out!"

Villagers peeked through their windows and out of alleys to investigate Solomon's disturbance. Curious onlookers spilled out of their homes and crowded around the market square. Tuesday, Zed, and their parents joined the new arrivals in loud exclamations of surprise and confusion before melting into the crowd and slipping away.

Mrs. Furst led them away from the market, weaving through a maze of alleys and side streets to avoid detection. It was slow going, with Tuesday steadying Zed with her one working arm and their father thumping along behind them on his crutch. Mrs. Furst went on ahead to check that their route was clear.

"Where are we heading, anyway?" Zed asked his mother as she motioned to them to follow her around a corner.

There was no answer. Zed and Tuesday shuffled around the corner to find a completely deserted alley.

"Hey, where did—" Mr. Furst asked, catching up to them. Beside him, Nyx bristled and growled before streaking up the alley and around another corner. Before anyone could stop her, Tuesday pelted down the alley after Nyx.

"Tuesday, don't!" Mr. Furst shouted, struggling to keep up with her.

Tuesday did.

When she finally caught up with Nyx she found her mother lying unconscious in the street at the center of a ring of blue flames. Nyx prowled in front of the protective circle, growling and snapping at the two Red Hand agents calmly backing up and pulling off their gloves. The agents glanced over at Tuesday, then back at Nyx. Inside the flaming barrier, Mrs. Furst sat up and shook her head.

In the moment it took Mrs. Furst to get her bearings, the Red Hand agents started in Tuesday's direction.

"Tuesday—run!" Mrs. Furst screamed. But it was already too late. In one fluid motion, without even interrupting his stride, one of the agents pulled a coiled length of cord from beneath his cloak and flicked it in Tuesday's direction. Weighted beads at each end whistled as the cord sailed through the air, then wound itself around Tuesday's ankles. Tuesday fell backward, struggling to free her legs.

SPLAT. Tuesday looked up. The agents looked down. Their feet were lodged in a mass of purple foam expanding rapidly toward their knees. In unison, they attempted to step away from the growing blob, but found their boots stuck. Solomon ran toward the agents from the opposite end of the alley, lobbing small purple orbs in their direction. The gluey grenades sprouted like mushrooms on the agents' arms and legs when they made contact.

The agents made no attempt to free themselves. They just stood there, following Solomon with detached stares as he rushed past to help Tuesday out of their snare. Mrs. Furst stood and walked unsteadily over to join him, escorted by Nyx.

"No matter," said one of the agents.

"We'll be seeing you again soon, Your Highness," said the other, with a bow.

It made a nice change of pace to ride on a hoversled without being tied up in a sack, Zed observed as Solomon drove them back to the base. He let his legs dangle off the back of the sled and gave his toes an experimental wriggle inside his sneakers. The feeling in his leg had mostly returned, although the pins-and-needles sensation had not quite subsided. Tuesday alternated stretching her fingers and clutching her fists, comparing the response of one hand to the other. Their parents sat between them in silence, each draping a protective arm over the shoulder of the nearest child as though they feared Zed and Tuesday might float away or evaporate into thin air if someone didn't hold onto them.

Nyx bounded alongside on foot, completely undeterred by the increasing steepness of the rocky slope leading up to the cave that formed the base's other secret entrance. While the waterfall entrance had been designed to mimic an abandoned hideout, this cave was bustling with uniformed workers stacking wooden crates of crystals and mushrooms along the walls. A supervisor handing out helmets and gloves to workers heading into the mine nodded to Solomon, who parked the sled and led his group through the security entrance behind her.

"Looks like we each have some things we need to fill the others in on," Solomon commented as he punched buttons and submitted to scans, finally standing aside and waving everyone in when the last set of doors parted to admit them. "I'm fascinated to see how the whole puzzle fits together, at last."

"Then you're not mad at us for taking off?" Zed asked as they made their way up the staircase at the end of the deserted corridor.

"Well, obviously that was a risky thing to do—the General and I were worried. When the General realized she didn't have a copy of the daily report, she asked to see mine, thinking there had been a printing error. But when your escorts reported you missing, she realized exactly where you'd gone and sent me to keep an eye on you. I wasn't expecting anything quite as dramatic as the events of this morning, of course, but 'all's well that ends well' I suppose."

"The General?" Mr. Furst interrupted. "So, this is the Resistance headquarters, then?" He shook his head with a bitter laugh. "There's irony for you."

"What? Why?" Tuesday demanded. "What's ironic? And—you know about the Resistance? I mean, we'd pretty much accepted that you knew about Falinnheim the whole time, being from the Legion and all, but—"

"The Legion?" Mr. Furst interrupted. "Where'd you get that idea? I was never with the Legion."

"But, your umbrella!" Tuesday protested. "All the soldiers have those transformy weapon things! And Nicodemus and those two soldiers at home said they knew you, and—"

Mr. Furst dropped to one knee so he could look his children in the eye. "I think we've all known, for longer than we were willing to admit, that you've suspected Mom and I kept some things from you. All will be explained. I just need you to know that everything we've had to do—it was because we love you and wanted to protect you. Obviously things got more complicated than we planned…I would have done anything to keep you out of danger, anything, and you got dragged into this anyway—" His voice caught in his throat.

Tuesday buried her face in her father's neck. Just this once, she decided, the answers could wait.

Nyx burrowed under Mr. Furst's arm, desperate to be part of the family moment. Tuesday was nearly knocked over as the dog pried her snout between them.

"Now, let's go meet this General," Mrs. Furst said brightly, wiping a tear from the corner of her eye. "We have a lot to talk about."

"Right after a trip to the medical ward," said Solomon. He led them out of the stairwell, down another hall, and into an office where a woman in white robes helped Mr. Furst onto a floating platform so she could examine his foot.

"Please wait here," Solomon instructed. "I need to report in, and Doctor Ubime will take good care of you in the meantime. I'll return shortly—I expect this is an interview the General will want to conduct personally."

After a brief examination, the doctor soaked Mr. Furst's foot in a pail of faintly brown liquid, which both relieved the pain and swelling and gave off a fragrance resembling root beer. She then wrapped the foot in yard after yard of cloth bandages and instructed Mr. Furst to keep weight off of it until he returned to her office the next day for bone scans.

While the doctor rummaged in an adjoining storage room for a pair of crutches, Solomon returned with the General at his heels.

"You children gave us quite a scare," she said, striding into the room, "but I suppose I should have expected your reaction, under the circumstances. At least now we can all get some ans—"

The General stopped as Mr. and Mrs. Furst stood to meet her. The color drained from her face. Solomon hastened to steady her as she took a tottering step backward.

"Beren…" she whispered.

"Mother?" exclaimed Mr. Furst.

"Mother?" Zed, Tuesday, and Solomon echoed.

"Mom, what's going on?" Zed asked, turning to Mrs. Furst.

"Mom?" The General repeated in disbelief. "This is your mother?"

"WHAT'S GOING ON?" Tuesday demanded.

"That's what I'd like to know," Solomon said with a shrug.

"I thought you were dead," the General breathed, cupping Mr. Furst's face in her hands. "How is this possible?"

"I'll explain everything, Mom," said Mr. Furst, wrapping the General in a hug. "But it looks like you'll have to fill me in too—how did you end up leading the Resistance?"

"How did you end up married to a princess?" the General countered, laughing and wiping her streaming eyes.

"A what?" said Tuesday.

"Children," Mr. Furst said, still clutching the General around the shoulder, "I'd like you to meet your grandmother."

Zed and Tuesday's mouths hung open. The General's face went pale again. And Solomon and Mrs. Furst had never worn broader smiles.

Chapter 27

LOOKING BACKWARD, MOVING FORWARD

An interview room simply wouldn't do for a family reunion of this magnitude—Solomon wouldn't hear of it. He conducted everyone to a pair of velvet sofas in the officers' lounge, then hurried off to see what he could plunder from the kitchens.

"You didn't start without me, did you?" he asked when he returned with a stack of dishes and a berry pie. "I want to hear everything."

Mr. Furst accepted a slice of pie and propped his bandaged foot up on the coffee table. "Kids, I have news," he began. "This may be hard to believe, given the events of the past week, but I actually am a security consultant."

"What?" Tuesday screeched.

Her father silenced her with a settle down gesture and continued. "However, when Mom and I left on that business trip, the 'business' was actually about my last job. Before I was a security consultant, I was a bodyguard. Mom's bodyguard, in fact."

"Wait, back up!" Tuesday protested. "Begin at the beginning!"

Mr. Furst took a moment to consider this. "There's so much to explain, and of course I don't know the whole story myself, but…I suppose 'the beginning' would be on the day your Mom and I met. As a young man I worked for the Royal Guard, the force tasked with securing the palace and protecting the royal family of Falinnheim—the Regents Council, they were called," he explained for Zed and Tuesday's benefit. "Sixteen years ago, a man named Tyrren plotted a takeover of the government. On the day his forces attacked the palace, I had been assigned to protect the most recently appointed member of the council: the Moderator's granddaughter, Princess Theadora. We managed to escape the palace, but there was nothing we could do to reverse the plan Tyrren had set in motion. The rest of the Regents Council was killed, along with anyone else who stood in Tyrren's way.

"I knew Tyrren would stop at nothing to eliminate any threat to his hold on power—and a surviving member of the rightful ruling body was a grave threat. I needed to find somewhere the princess would be safe. By chance, we met a man who claimed to have a device that could transport people to other spaces—places that exist outside of Falinnheim. Legend has it that the ancient founders of Falinnheim originally came from this other space, in fact. I didn't really believe in the old legends of course, but somehow or other, this device actually worked."

"Oh, I never doubted Scrimbley," Mrs. Furst cut in.

Tuesday was about to voice her opinion on that point, but Zed shot her a warning glare—they'd never get through the whole story if they got sidetracked.

Mr. Furst continued. "He sent us somewhere we hoped Tyrren would never be able to find us. He kept in contact, updating us on major developments from time to time, but it soon became clear that if we returned, we'd be signing our own death warrants. So, we stayed. We changed our names and did our best to blend in with an unfamiliar society. At first, our relationship was strictly based on my professional duty to protect the princess, but in time it became...something more."

Mrs. Furst took his hand, lacing their fingers together as she took up the narration. "We got married, found jobs, bought a house. Then you children came along. In short, we built an entirely new life together. But we never lost hope that someday the time would be right for us to return to Falinnheim and help those that had been left behind. And last week, we got a message from Scrimbley that convinced us the time had come."

"How was he able to communicate with you?" the General inquired. "Has Scrimbley been traveling to this other world to visit you?"

"Oh no, nothing like that," Mr. Furst answered. "He just sent messages—with this." He reached into his pocket and produced a flattened metal ball, split down the middle along a hinged seam, almost like a pocket watch or—Tuesday sucked in her breath as she recognized it—a compass.

"Scrimbley's device and ours formed a set. Messages could be sent directly from one to the other by inscribing on the inside surface of the lid; whatever was written on one would show up on the other until read and erased."

He handed the device to the General and Solomon to examine. "Think of it as a cross between an Etch A Sketch and a fax machine," he explained to Zed and Tuesday.

While the adults inspected the mysterious object, Tuesday whispered to Zed out of the corner of her mouth. "What's an…etchy-sketch?"

"No idea," Zed whispered back. "What's a fax machine?"

Tuesday shrugged.

"Scrimbley's message said a representative of the Resistance had contacted him, hoping to meet with us," Mrs. Furst continued.

"Not 'us', Thea," Mr. Furst corrected. "You."

The General's brow furrowed.

"We knew it was possible that this meeting was not set up by Resistance agents at all, but wanted to investigate, just in case," explained Mrs. Furst. "We arranged to have Scrimbley transport us back to Falinnheim earlier than this agent wanted to meet so we could check the situation out. We quickly realized the whole thing had been orchestrated by Tyrren's spies, hoping to flush us out of hiding. But before we could make it back to Scrimbley and go home, two soldiers had already beat us there. Scrimbley got you away from the soldiers, but he knew that the imposter Resistance agent would be arriving soon. You couldn't stay there, and you couldn't go home, so he thought you'd be better off hiding somewhere else. We, meanwhile, had two separate groups tracking our movements, so we couldn't go get you ourselves—that would have put you in even more danger. It's a good thing we left Nyx with you while we were gone—I can't imagine how you would have escaped from those soldiers without her."

Tuesday couldn't resist any longer. "Wait, Nyx! You didn't explain about Nyx—how did you get a Gabriel Hound?"

"That's a tale in itself, but for now it's enough to say that we brought her with us from Falinnheim on the day we left. Dad couldn't be with me every moment, so Nyx provided an extra layer of security."

"How did the soldiers know where to find us?" Zed asked. "And why were they so interested in Dad?"

"That's a part of the story I'm not sure on, myself," said Mr. Furst. "From what we've been able to gather, after the revolution the members of the Royal Guard that sided with Tyrren were transferred to the Legion, for some reason. Not all soldiers in the Legion used to be in the Royal Guard, but those that were are bitter that the revolution didn't end up benefiting them in the way they had hoped, and vengeful against anyone who didn't go along with their plot in the first place. They view my decision to protect your mother instead of pledge loyalty to the other guards as a betrayal."

"So the Red Hand wants to capture the last member of the Regents Council and finish what Tyrren started sixteen years ago," the General summarized, gesturing to Mrs. Furst. "And the guards who turned against the Regents Council are determined to punish you for resisting their plan," she concluded with a nod at her son.

"How did either of them figure out how to find you?" Solomon asked. "It sounds like neither the Red Hand nor the Legion knew what the other group was up to."

"Only Scrimbley knows the answer to that." Mr. Furst scowled. "And if I ever get my hands on that scoundrel again, I intend to find out."

"You're being too hard on him!" Mrs. Furst scolded her husband. "He helped us escape Falinnheim in the first place, he's kept us informed all these years—and don't forget he rescued the children!"

"For a price," he muttered back. "Everything he's done has either been out of greed or cowardice."

"Scrimbley may have some…unconventional business strategies," said Mrs. Furst, "but deep down I think his heart is in the right place. He has a good conscience, it's just that…well, let's just say his moral compass doesn't always point north."

"So, while we were in New Angkor, you went back to Scrimbley, but found out his device was broken," Zed clarified.

"Right," said Mrs. Furst. "We didn't know exactly where you were, and we couldn't reveal ourselves to you until we managed to throw the spies off our trail. We thought the Red Hand probably didn't know you even existed, and we wanted to keep things that way. So, I came up with some clues for you to follow, clues I knew no one from Falinnheim would be able to decipher. I told Nyx where to find each message as you went along, and she helped steer you to the right locations. We were hoping to guide you to Kyoto and meet up with you there. We had heard the Resistance was based somewhere nearby and figured even if the initial meeting that brought us here was a trap, maybe we could make contact with the real Resistance anyway."

"Wait, Nyx led us to all the nursery rhymes?" Tuesday asked. "And what do you mean, you 'told' her where they were?"

"Well, as you've figured out by now, Nyx is not an ordinary dog," Mrs. Furst explained. "Each Gabriel Hound chooses a person, and they form a sort of bond that's difficult to explain. As Nyx's person, I'm able to communicate with her."

"NYX CAN TALK?" Tuesday gasped.

"Oh no, don't be silly!" Mrs. Furst laughed. "I know you've seen her do some amazing things this week, but animals can't talk."

"But then how—" Zed asked.

"She's telepathic," Mrs. Furst responded casually, taking another bite of her pie.

Mr. Furst rolled his eyes. Zed, Tuesday and the General looked incredulous. Solomon wore the expression of someone who had just unwrapped a particularly delightful birthday present.

"Of course, animals don't think in words, exactly," Mrs. Furst continued, ignoring their reactions. "Mostly we can sense one another's emotions. But if I concentrate very hard, we're able to share brief mental images—in this case, I showed her the places I'd left you a message. And of course, it didn't matter if you found every single one—you just needed enough of a pattern to realize that you weren't alone, and that you should follow Nyx's lead. And I must say, you did remarkably well! If you hadn't been captured by the Legion on the way to Kyoto, the plan would have worked flawlessly!"

"It was really Solomon who captured us," Zed pointed out. "The Legion couldn't get past Nyx."

Mrs. Furst smiled and gave Nyx's ears an affectionate scritch.

"Well, all things considered, that's probably the best thing that could have happened," said Mr. Furst. "You were safe from the Legion, and in the end, we got to meet with the Resistance, just like we'd planned."

"What about the fake message in Kyoto, then?" Zed asked.

"While you were staying here at the base, we were waiting for you in Kyoto. We didn't know exactly where you were, but from what I could sense from Nyx I knew you were safe, and not that far away. So we just waited," his mother explained. "Unfortunately, it seems this delay gave the Red Hand time to pick up on some of the rhymes we'd left behind. They had no way to decode the messages of course, so it looks like they set up a decoy to see who would come along to read it. Perhaps if we'd met up earlier, they wouldn't have noticed the nursery rhymes…but then, if you hadn't met Solomon, we wouldn't have known how to contact the Resistance."

"No point in what-ifs," Mr. Furst concluded. "We're all back together now—that's what's important."

They talked all morning, sharing all the stories they'd missed in their separation. The General recounted her perspective of the day of Tyrren's attack—how word had seeped out from the capital in Alexandria to the surrounding cities and villages, the shock and outrage of the people blindsided by the loss of their revered monarchs, her own despair when her husband and son had not come home, her escape into the mountains with Obaachan, and how this had steeled her resolve to take matters into her own hands. Solomon's tale, of leading a protest movement in a small coastal village before the General recruited him, was especially gripping, as Tuesday and Zed had not heard any of it before. They shared tears over the memory of family and friends killed in the attack or captured in the years since; they laughed over recollections of happier times together; they even gossiped and griped over Tyrren's failure to feed the poor and maintain the roads as well as the Regents Council had done.

"But now that Princess Theadora has returned," Solomon said, beaming at Mrs. Furst, "the Resistance can begin a new chapter in Falinnheim's history and return the people to peace and prosperity once more."

Zed was surprised to notice the change in his mother's expression as Solomon spoke—all the relief and contentment seemed to leak out of her like a deflating balloon. She sat in silence, her gaze losing its focus while she absently fingered the delicate gold chain peeking out from the neck of her cloak.

"Of course, many who lived in Alexandria or had dealings with the Regents Council will recognize you," the General said, "but there are those that will want proof of your identity."

Mrs. Furst pulled the long chain out of her robes, unclasped the ends, and slid off the two rings that hung there. She slipped her wedding ring back onto its accustomed finger; on the index finger of her other hand she placed a larger gold ring the children had never seen before. She held up her hand to show the others its flat face, engraved with an image of two intertwined birds.

"The royal seal should be enough to satisfy anyone's doubts," said Mr. Furst. "When the ring is worn by anyone other than the person it was created for, the image on the seal disappears, so it can't be used by an imposter."

Solomon seemed to sense the melancholy shift the room's atmosphere had taken. He pulled a glass ball out of his pocket and made a great show of consulting it. "The morning has gotten away from us—it's nearly time for the afternoon shift to begin work!" he said, standing.

"Obaachan will never let me hear the end of it if I'm late for our lunch appointment," the General agreed. "Although perhaps she'll let it slide just this once, considering the surprise that will come with it. Come," she said, helping her son to his crutches, "you know how she hates to be kept waiting!"

Everyone filed out of the room, but Tuesday and Zed held back a moment to talk with their mother alone. She raised her arms and tucked them in on either side, each nestled beneath a wing of her cloak.

"Mom?" Tuesday ventured. "About what Solomon said—about you being secret royalty, and proving who you are, and joining the Resistance…"

Mrs. Furst looked solemn. "We'll have to discuss that," she said heavily.

"It's just…I was hoping, now that we're all back together again, and Dad has another one of Scrimbley's devices, we'd be able to…you know, go home. Go back to normal."

"Normal," Mrs. Furst chuckled bitterly. "Normal is relative." She sighed and pulled her children closer. "Nothing about our life has really ever been normal. 'Home' is relative too—after all, returning to Falinnheim was coming home, for me. But if you mean going back to the other world…I'm afraid that isn't possible. At least, not right now. Dad may have one half of Scrimbley's device, but unfortunately it was Scrimbley's that controlled the actual transporting. They work as a set—a transmitter and a receiver. If Scrimbley's is broken, then our half is useless."

"Even if we could go back," Zed realized aloud, "we'd have a lot of explaining to do once we got there. We've all been missing for a week with no explanation.

And our house is probably a wreck, after Nyx fended off those soldiers. Someone probably called the police when none of us showed up for school or work for a few days. No one would believe what really happened if we told them, and there's no excuse we could make up that would explain it all."

Tuesday bit her lip and tried to blink away the emotions welling up behind her eyes. "There's still so much I don't know! How did you escape from the palace with Dad? And how did you know where to find Scrimbley, and where did Nyx come from, and—"

"What were you and Dad up to while we were following your messages?" Zed chimed in. "And how were you able to post the messages without anyone recognizing you? And speaking of the messages, how did you hack into the holograms' programming in Persepolis? In fact—how did you come up with the idea to use nursery rhymes in the first place?"

"Well, since we can't go back anytime soon, it looks like we have all the time in the world to tell those stories," their mother answered. "And there's so much about Falinnheim I want to show you! Even though things here have gotten a bit complicated, Falinnheim is still an amazing place. I can't wait to show you all the things I've missed about my home."

Tuesday sniffled and cleared her throat. "Well, I guess there are some dodos I've been meaning to go see."

"And I definitely can't leave until I learn how those holograms work," said Zed.

"You don't even know the half of it," their mother assured them. "There's magic hiding behind the normal for anyone who takes the time to look. I've spent the last sixteen years discovering the everyday magic of the other world. Now it's my turn to share the magic of Falinnheim with you."

Zed tucked his arm around his mother's elbow and shot Tuesday an encouraging smile. She wiped her eyes and nodded back.

"We better get going," he said. "We have a lunch appointment with Obaachan—and you know how she hates to be kept waiting."